Prolance

Copyright © 2017 I. Ashmawey

www.prolancewriting.com
California, USA

ISBN: 978-0-9987527-8-5

STORIES THAT ARE SHORT

VOL I

a collection of 5-minute short stories
to read before turning on the tv

by
I. Ashmawey

Table of Contents

Dedication

This book is dedicated to all who love to read.

But it is also, more importantly, dedicated
to my friend and beloved wife, Angie, who
listened to every 'story that is short' in this
book, even the ones that put her to sleep.

Read!

... and let the words guide your way.

Introduction

People don't read anymore.

Some people say they do, but I differ with them on what classifies as reading. To read the headline of an article and say you've read it, that's just not right. To watch a five-minute summary video online and claim to have read "The Art of War," well that's just even more not right. The most not right, however, is being truly oblivious to the benefits of reading.

I'm particularly referring to fiction. To be able to imagine the unimaginable is a gift we humans possess, one that we take for granted. You see, the moment you imagine something, the moment your mushy brain is able to concoct such an absurdly ridiculous idea, the moment ink stains paper and the words are written, that ridiculously impossible idea becomes destined to come alive.

This is a book of very, very short stories. They will each take you no longer than five minutes to read. Keep it next to your couch, lazy boy recliner, bed, or toilet. Before you watch TV, just read one short story and have your spirit fly to another land. For just five minutes.

1

Star Bright

I. Ashmawey

Adam Casswell appeared genuinely sanguine as he sat at the witness stand. He wore a 24-carat smile; not one of sarcasm, but rather content. The judge grimaced every time he glanced and saw Casswell's curled lips, cool and confident. But his unclouded serenity was out of his hands. Whether he would be set free or sent up the river, he would be satisfied.

He took off his thick brown frames and rubbed the lenses with his beige, passé, tweed jacket. As soon as the glasses rested on his nose once again, he went directly back to smiling.

Adam Casswell wasn't old, but atop his head lay a glistening gray blanket. He liked to think of it as a sign of wisdom.

The judge shifted in his mahogany leather seat as he continued flipping through the case documentation on his tablet.

"Your crime," the judge began before clearing his throat, "is immeasurable. It pains me to even be aware of such a case, let alone be the presiding judge on the matter." Though the words were harsh, Casswell's smile wasn't affected. I couldn't take my eyes off him; genial and majestically calm. What was he thinking? Feeling? Of the many arduous cases I had witnessed as a Courtroom Guard, this was the most bewitching. For the first time in my profession, I imagined being in the defendant's shoes, waiting painfully to have my fate handed to me. What must this have been like a few hundred years ago when the death penalty was still in effect? The ominous "guilty" uttered by a judge must have had a disparate meaning when the gallows were the outcome.

Though, I never understood how that was deemed a punishment. After all, death cuts a life short and one does not endure any forfeiture. The way the judicial system resolved things today was true punishment. To be chastised; ostracized from a community and exiled for the remainder of your days. Seemed more decorous to me. Of course, the final result was still death since most convicts wouldn't survive more than a few weeks alone. We just didn't see them wither away and die. I think this offended us less.

"Adam Casswell, while I have respect for your knowledge and education, the hatred I have for your crime trumps all. You purposefully and callously broke the number one law we have sworn to uphold as a nation. You are thusly convicted." With those words, a cold fear made it's way across every chest in the courtroom.

Though many in the audience venerated this man, most of them intently looked away, murmuring to themselves. They didn't want to be connected to him, not even by sight. Perhaps not looking helps convince us bad things aren't happening. If a tree falls in a forest...

Personally, I had a visceral respect for Dr. Casswell. How could I not? The first man in over a century to complete a doctorate degree. And to add to the controversy, rather than studying online, Casswell chose a brick and mortar university— one that had been decommissioned for decades. As such, Dr. Casswell was the only student and the only teacher. He was also the groundskeeper, the janitor, the cook, etc. He spent long truculent nights in the barren, decrepit libraries putting pen to paper and ink to mind. Nevertheless, despite the eccentricities, Dr. Casswell was indisputably the most educated and also the most intelligent person on the planet. It was not an exaggeration to say he was a walking dictionary, an encyclopedia, a beacon of knowledge.

"We will recess before sentencing," the judge said, banging his gavel.

I sat alone in the cafeteria and devoured a French dip sandwich. Oddly, I found myself wondering about my sandwich's name. I pulled out my phone and quickly searched 'French dip'. The results: how to make French dip, nearest locations serving French dip, more French dip recipes, and French dip merchandise for some reason. I guess I shouldn't complain, I owned a Sriracha sauce t-shirt. But where was the history of the name French dip? I sunk my teeth into the soggy bread and piping hot jus dripped down my chin.

I bet Dr. Casswell knew the origin.

Dr. Adam Casswell. Phone still in my hand, I googled his name. How could such a great man make such a grievous mistake? What was his story? No social media presence, no interviews. All I found was what others had written about him. His biography, his family, his studies, his career. I quickly scanned the headlines. Within a few seconds, I felt I had a good understanding of his history. But nothing I saw explained why he had decided to break the law.

Naturally, many people began questioning the legitimacy of his Ph.D. as surely, a man who could brazenly break such a law could lie about anything. These were the same people who from the beginning claimed no one was capable of producing a doctorate degree in today's day and age. It was quite an amazing feat and not easily accepted by the public. From the day Dr. Casswell announced he would pursue this undertaking, he received attacks ranging from insults to death threats of the most draconian nature. It's not that people were against knowledge, of course not. Rather, humanity had simply evolved beyond the stage of academic exploration.

Most people, particularly the ones who vehemently fought Dr. Casswell, argued that in order to progress, one must invent things that were befitting of their era. Not simply study for the sake of studying as Dr. Casswell did.

The first wheel was invented for pottery—surprisingly not chariots—in Mesopotamia around 3500 BC. And since then, we have been revolutionizing tools to make our lives easier. At first, our tools grew larger and more sophisticated; this was the industrial age. Then our tools became smaller and even more sophisticated; the technical age. Then our tools gathered large quantities of data—all knowledge; the information age. Knowledge that for centuries took patience to acquire was now easily accessible within seconds. Having access to all this data made us realize not all data was needed, relevant, or even valid. Information alone was overrated.

We haven't had another 'age' of any sort since. Then again, these titles are only given after the fact. Maybe our children will know what our age was called. Maybe.

But Dr. Casswell. Why?

My phone vibrated with a text—they were ready for sentencing. I swallowed the rest of my arbitrarily named sandwich and rushed to the courtroom. I was nervous. So much so that my heart shook in my hollow chest. What was going to happen to this man? This smart, intelligent, noble pioneer? Why did he do what he did? He must have had a reason.

He must have.

"Adam Casswell, you have been convicted of sky gazing," the judge spat vehemently. The crowd in the courtroom shuddered. The mere thought of looking up to the sky brought chills to the strongest of spines. How did his neck even bend far enough to look up? And worse, to see that terrifying chasm? Those who had tried in the past paid dearly. And over the centuries, hardly anyone thought about it anymore. After all, sky gazing was a rather difficult affair. The majority of inhabitable dwellings on the planet were entirely covered. One must travel vast distances to come close to even catching a glimpse. And that's all Dr. Casswell was able to do anyway, catch a glimpse.

The judge asked if Dr. Casswell had anything to say before his sentencing. His smile *still* sat comfortably on his dignified visage. He rose from his seat quickly and with resolution. For a middle aged man, his motions were swift. Every cell phone in the courtroom pointed towards Dr. Casswell, including mine, and began recording.

"There was once a mouse born in captivity," he began. He spoke slowly. Oh, so slowly. But his voice was clear and strong. Everybody listened and no one dared miss a letter.

"Was this your mouse, Mr. Casswell?" the judge asked, ignoring the doctor's Ph.D.

"No. By no means was it mine."

"Clerk, verify this mouse," the judge ordered. The judge even pulled out his own cell phone and searched 'Mouse born in captivity.' He scrolled through the results as Casswell spoke.

"This mouse, from before it could open its eyes, was confined to a box. Closed from every side," Casswell continued.

"Wait, how can it breathe? The mouse needs to be able to breathe!" the judge screamed as he stood up from his seat.

"Surely, all will make sense," Casswell assured. The judge slowly lowered himself again. "The mouse lived just fine. Every night when it fell asleep, someone lifted the top of the box and gifted a piece of cheese for the next day." The judge nodded his head in approval. "The mouse believed it was living a perfect, most optimal life. Things could not possibly get any better. A roof over its head, warmth, comfort, and guaranteed nourishment. Years later, a hole was poked in the box. Just a hole, nothing larger than the size of a pin. What happened next was unfounded. The mouse could not stay put. Scratching, gnawing, chewing. And after years of captivity, the mouse broke free from the box and was welcomed by an unexplored world!" Casswell's smile grew. "You see, the hole gave the mouse something unprecedented, and nothing could equate it."

"What did it give, Mr. Casswell? Air? Is this is the explanation for how the mouse could breathe in the box?" the judge asked.

"No, your honor," Casswell responded. "Curiosity. Knowing there was much to be discovered created an illness—an addiction if you will—to discover. And curiosity, your honor, curiosity, my friends, is not easily curable." The crowd was silent. "Actually, there is no cure."

The judge's face turned red with anger. He knew what Dr. Casswell was trying to do. "Mr. Casswell. Did you or did you not gaze at the sky?"

"I did."

"And did that or did that not influence your academic progress?"

"It made all the difference," Dr. Casswell responded.

"As such, you will be stripped of your degree. Moreover, I hereby sentence you to exile. You shall be ostracized and spurned in our traditional fashion. Adam Casswell, you will be written in history as a criminal."

"You're too late, your honor," Casswell spoke.

"Too late for what?"

"The seed of curiosity has been planted in every able mind in this courtroom. It's up to each farmer whether or not they will grow it."

Six months later, I had reached the end. The corridor was narrow, barely large enough to fit me. I was surrounded by stone walls from every direction except behind me. Clearly, I had reached the terminus of the path. I began hammering the wall above. I had traveled so long and so far, not knowing if I'd ever reach the end. Or if there was an end to begin with. But this was it.

It took days to make even a dent in the stone, but after a week of hammering, I finally poked a hole above me. That hole, that tiny infinitesimal aperture, that breach of freedom and reform, gave me a surge of energy I cannot describe. In that second, I understood the mouse. We were connected.

Not long after, the ceiling came tumbling down. Though my body ached as I watched the stones fall, I was no longer tired. Truthfully, the most difficult part of the journey was getting up to take my first steps.

Unlike what I had imagined I would do next, I did not slowly or gradually raise my head. Rather, my neck that had comfortably faced downward for my entire life immediately tilted and gazed to the heavens. How quickly we can evolve when motivated. Within seconds of peering into the open abyss decorated with floating lights, within seconds of realizing the sheer massiveness of the universe, within seconds of understanding the brevity of our existence, hundreds of questions flooded my mind. No answers, just questions.

And I vowed to answer every one of them.

Even if I died trying.

I. Ashmawey

2

The Subtle Overwhelming Differences Between Jupiterians and Humans
~ an essay ~

I. Ashmawey

The Jupiterians call me Falak. They never hid from me the fact that I was human. Not that they could have had they tried; missing three eyes stood out like a sore thumb. Oh, not to mention the fact that I had thumbs. At the very least, I shared with them a Jupiteroid body shape and a similar consistent softness to the skin. I never truly noticed the extents of the differences however until the day I visited Earth after twenty years of being on Jupiter. I don't believe any of the Jupiterians noticed either; unless they did but never said anything.

I must make one thing perfectly clear: I was not kidnapped—the Jupiterians saved me. My birth parents abandoned me in a forest in Waukegan, Illinois in the early summer of Earth's 2007. A group of Jupiterians were on a routine Observing Trek, annual trips they had been conducting to Earth for over seven centuries. They typically cloak their aircrafts using mental practices and hover over the surface of the planet by several miles. After a week of hovering, they would then transport down to Earth and cloak themselves with the same practice used on their aircrafts. They would then roam amongst humans for thirty days, since that's a time good for any observance, or any practice, or anything really.

It just so happened that on that trip in 2007, on that particular day, a Jupiterian female by the name of Uva crossed my path. Uva, who would later become my adopted mother, was exploring the forest and paying particularly close attention to the pine trees, for their smell was one of her favorite scents. Suddenly, she heard my feeble cry. I was hungry, which she instinctively took care of immediately. Rules, regulations, and etiquette of Observing suddenly flew out the window. While the Jupiterians are a peaceful people and not at all disregarding, it was a conscious decision they had made never to interfere with a species. Whether it was masses of a species killing each other, or one lone individual in need of help, the rule was absolute. For if they helped one, they would have to help all. But as fate would have it, Uva would hear my whimper, see my face, experience a hominid weakness, and sneak me back on their aircraft. Some protested after I arrived on Jupiter, but nothing serious. I live a most happy life; meditative, purposeful, and peaceful.

On my twentieth birthday, I was asked to join the annual Observing Trek to

I. Ashmawey

Earth. As a native human brought up on Jupiter, the Jupiterian Council felt I would give an interesting perspective and asked me to document three differences I would observe between Jupiterians and Humans. Of course, there were more than three. But when looking at the most prominent three, do the others really matter?

It is on the eve of my last night on Earth that I scribe my findings. I am writing two copies of this essay, one in mental recording for Jupiter, and the other in English digital format for humans, in hopes that it be found someday and may perchance be of benefit.

The First Difference

To date, humans believe that they have had three worldwide conflicts. It is, in fact, more than three. But during the other wars, historical record keeping was, and still is, rather primitive. Today much more is being recorded than before, but generally things of no value. Most humans believe, as Jupiterians do, in a Supreme Being. The Supreme Being's teachings are organized in a religion. Unlike Jupiterians though, humans are ironically willing to disobey the Beings laws in His name. As such, the first documented world war was fought in the name of religion.

The second was fought on bigotry, that is belief that one physical attribute is more superior to another. The third was fought on hate.

Of course, each of these wars perpetuated false reasons for beginning. The first, ownership of land. The second, ownership of weapons. The third, ownership of energy.

The first main difference between Jupiterians and Humans is the need for conflict. They began their species fighting each other over sustenance when there was always enough for all. And until today, on an individual level, you will find them fighting in the streets over a vehicle parking spot or due to conflict with mating rituals. This is actual fighting, mind you. Physical altercation that may result in pain and possible damages. And on a group level, they completely annihilate each other. They kill millions of innocent lives and then continue on their day, eating, drinking, and sleeping. Yes, they sleep after doing so. Can you believe this? The first difference is the largest difference. They have not yet evolved as to settle differences using the gift of speech. Many have not spoken in years. This leads us to the second difference.

The Second Difference

Humans do not speak to one another. The average human will wake up to their devices, work on their devices, purchase materials and sustenance on their devices, entertain by use of their devices, learn from their devices, most will befriend and only befriend their devices, and sleep by their devices. They further use their devices to bathe, recreate, debate, relax; there is not a single act that humans do without use of their devices.

This, of course, leads humans to never speak to one another. Some lie to themselves and say they do, but they do not. They speak through their devices to fake personas created by others. It used to be that people fake relationships behind their devices. But now it is the devices that fake them almost entirely by anticipating the responses and then responding for them. Humans now spend the majority of their time entertaining, either by watching simulated sports, playing in a virtual reality, or watching other people living. Those who watch, pay. Those who perform, charge.

This way of living leads to humans becoming strangers. Even amongst family, in one household, they do not speak or hear each other. They all live with devices in their ears and on their eyes. They sustain themselves alone and sleep alone. They have overlooked what Jupiterians knew and understood from the dawn of time: we were created to know one another. For not knowing, leads to hate. Never mind all the benefits of knowing others: spiritual enlightenment, knowledge, broadening horizons, etc. It would be more than enough simply to not hate. But humans have such an ego that they do not believe they have anything to learn from one another. And this leads us to my final point.

The Third Difference

Humans have an ego to rival any being in the explored universe. It is nothing Jupiterians have ever come across and I do not believe we shall ever encounter such an illness again. They have such an ego that they have created the name 'human' for themselves. Earthlings or Terrans was not good enough. This ego manifests in a general belief that existence revolves around them. While as a species they have gone through understandings of the great demotions, such as the world not being the center of the Galaxy, on an individual level they are rather doomed.

The reason humans spend so much time in leisure is that they believe they have nothing more to learn. The reason they believe this is because they receive pseudo-knowledge. This is in the form of bytes, one sentence blurbs that give no information, are incredibly misleading, and often manipulative. But due to the simple mindedness of humans, they cannot comprehend anything more. It is one thing to be uneducated, it is another to not *know* you are. As such, humans have become empty shells. No spirit, no mind, and no purpose. Vessels that require food and drink, and excrete what they take in.

Even on a personal, inter-social level, humans' egos do not allow them to be at fault. They cannot bear to admit mistakes to others, and this leads to continued furthering from each other, which is the second difference, and this leads to further fighting, which is the first difference.

Moreover, they cannot even bear to blame themselves secretly. If one does not have what they desire in life, they blame others for their situations. Rather than attempting to pursue their desires, they instead spend an entire lifetime blaming others. This is most baffling, as the blaming never results in happiness. But yet, that is what they choose to do.

Conclusion

The Jupiterian Council has graciously offered me the option of remaining on Earth. My family can easily be tracked or I can start a family of my own. Blending in should not be difficult. I have decided however to return back to Jupiter where my mind, body, and soul are evolved and enlightened.

Back home on Jupiter, I have my true family. Beings that love one another, speak to one another, tolerate each other's differences, learn from each other, and live lives filled with purpose and meaning. Even our entertainment is meaningful and recreative. I long for my home. And the best I can do is hope that humans one day, some day, seek more for their lives.

3

Five Minute Colors

I. Ashmawey

H er name was Noor. At the velvet age of fifteen, she stood in line—back straight—awaiting her turn. She pushed back her long, wavy, black hair to uncover her eyes.

Noor would have five minutes.

It can be said that her life built up to this moment. But in reality, it was this moment that would build the rest of her life. She took a step forward, following the fifteen-year-old in front of her. One step closer to her turn. Her pulse elevated; she could feel her heartbeat in her flushed cheeks. Her eyes like full moons and her mind racing, trying to calculate all the possible scenarios.

There would be only three possible colors to choose from. Which three, she did not know yet. She would only find out when she entered the Decision Room. There, she would have five minutes to choose which color she would be for the rest of her life. No changes can be made later.

Another step forward, and another step closer to her turn. She tried ranking all the colors in her head; a first favorite, second favorite, third. But it was so hard to choose! What color you were, as everyone knew, would be the number one indicator of your persona. It would be how the world perceived you. In essence, who you were, and your purpose, would all be defined by your color.

The line was long ahead of her. Noor tilted her head to the side to look ahead... very long. She turned her head and looked behind her; even longer. A long, straight line with thousands of fifteen-year-olds waiting to determine who they would be for the rest of their lives.

Standing in this line, it was difficult for Noor to feel special. Hundreds of thousands just like her. And let's be honest, that was just one year. The year before, there were hundreds of thousands as well. And the year before that, for many, many centuries. Not to mention the years to come, all would be the same. She was one person, one spec of sand on an eternal beach. But to her, this moment was everything.

As, again, she was sure the person in front of her felt.

And the person behind her.

Another step forward.

Suddenly, she heard a sound. A sound, any sound, was out of the ordinary. But this sound in particular! It was a man, an old man. He was screaming something but it was difficult to discern. She flexed her ears till she heard…

"Any color! Any color at all! Any color!" he screamed. Then she saw him. A haggard, old man with long, coarse, white hair laying unkempt on his shoulders. The man was red. It was the first thing Noor noticed when she saw him and because of that, she immediately had an understanding of who he was. He was running from the front of the line, which Noor couldn't see very well, towards the back of it. His arms flailing around, saying the same thing over and over. "Any color! Any color, children! Please listen to me!"

"What are you saying?" Noor whispered to herself.

The fifteen-year-old boy in front of her turned around. "Any color. My parents warned me this lunatic would be here. He's a crazy guy; he thinks you can be any color. Apparently, he does this every year."

That didn't make sense to Noor. Why would he do this year after year? There was only one way to find out.

Only one way, and only one chance.

She watched the man get closer and closer as he made his way down the line. "Any color!" he continued to scream. The majority of those in line looked the other way. It wasn't that he was ugly, it was simply their way of disassociating themselves from him. Don't look at him, and he can't affect you. Clearly, many others had been warned as well.

Noor wasn't warned though. And this made her want to explore.

The man got closer as he continued to run towards the back of the line. And Noor got closer as she took sporadic steps forward, her eyes fixated on him. Until finally, he came close enough to hear her ask, "Why?" The old man, just past Noor, paused in his tracks. It took him a moment before he finally turned to see Noor's face, flushed. She took a step away from him.

"I don't mean to frighten you, young lady. Not at all. It's just that no one has ever spoken to me in all my years of doing this."

Noor felt a bit better. She didn't feel he was dangerous. She felt comfortable enough to step back into the line. The line, which, everyone standing in had now turned away from looking even at Noor, for she had associated herself with the nutcase. "Why are you doing this?"

"Because I must warn you, dear girl. I must warn all of you," he responded.

"But if you know no one will listen, why do you do this every year?" Noor asked. She was to the point, but still polite. And she genuinely wanted to know.

The old man didn't like her question though. His face became blank, with an almost saddened look. "I'll answer your question, dear girl. I'll answer it. But pray, you first answer a question for me." Noor nodded in agreement. "Splendid. Why are you asking me about the reason I come here, instead of asking me about the content of my words?"

The question took Noor by surprise. She had assumed the old red man would ask her about herself, which color she would choose to be, or something of the sort. It's what all older people asked her. Moreover, the question confused her because she didn't know. She had no idea why it was that she didn't even think about what the man was saying. She only cared about why he decided to do something so strange and out of the ordinary.

"Honestly, I don't know. But I guess…" She thought for a second. "Okay, fine. I'll ask you about the content of your words. What is it you're saying? Any color?"

"Yes. Any color. You can be any color you want," he responded, with an inkling of a smile on his face.

"Yes, we have three choices," she commented.

"No, no, no, my dear!" He scrunched his face. He sighed before getting all his energy back and jumping to his tippy toes. "You can be… any… color. There is no limit to your choices."

"We can be any color?"

"Yes! Any color on the rainbow spectrum! And if you don't find the color you want, make your own! Heck, have no color! Or multiple colors!" The man was screaming by that point. He jumped up and down with every word, his smile reaching ear to ear. Finally! In all his years doing this, someone was listening! Or at least even acknowledging him.

"Okay, sir, let's not get carried away. No one can have no color!" she said with a chuckle. "And to have multiple colors, what would one even look like?! No, no. Let's take a step back."

"Listen to me, young one. I've seen it. Do you think I was always red?"

"Wait, now you're telling me you can change colors too?" she asked.

"I was blue. Then I was green. At one point, I was black and turquoise. At another, I had no color. As of two years ago, I was nutmeg," he told her.

"That's not even a color," the boy in front of Noor scolded before quickly turning back to face ahead.

"Well, it wasn't. But I made it. And I liked it," the old man responded. The person behind Noor in line nudged her forward. She took a few steps forward to catch up. The man followed her, walking backward.

"If what you say is true, why are you the only one to say this?" Noor asked.

"You're a smart cookie," he responded. "But you're still not asking the right questions. Nevertheless, I'll answer. I'm not the only one to say it. Many have said it for thousands of years. But people don't listen."

I. Ashmawey

"But wouldn't our parents have told us this if it were true? I know my parents love me, they would have warned me."

"I suspect your parents have yet to learn this themselves. They will eventually. By the time they get to my age, they will know. And then, who knows, perhaps they will be the ones coming to warn the youngsters. If only anyone listened."

Noor thought to herself. What if it was a lie? What if the whole system was just a lie? What if they had set it up in a way that you have to choose one color, and they tell you you must pick from the choices available, but you can actually pick any color?

Or… worse.

What if there was no lie, but rather people just thought things were the way they were? Simply because no one really asked.

Okay, this was all too confusing. Noor shook her head. No, no, no. She had a life to live. She wasn't going to waste it by making a mistake with choosing her color which would eventually ruin her entire existence. Plus, who wanted more than one color anyway? What are we, peacocks? No, thank you.

"Thank you, sir. But I'd rather…" And then she paused. Would she rather? Truly, would she rather just be normal? Like all the rest? Or would she rather… maybe… do something different? She looked at he long line; so many people all the same.

The person behind her nudged her again. She was getting close now, time had passed so quickly. She was only a few turns away. She saw the small, white, building in front of her where people went in, devoid of color, and came out freshly painted. The door opened and a fifteen-year-old came out, blue. The next person went in. Noor stepped forward.

"Okay, how will I know?" she asked the old man, now in a hurry. "How will I know which color I should be?"

"That's easy. The color you love, my dear," he responded. "And I'm glad you're finally asking the right questions."

"But what if I don't know which color I love?" she asked, as he followed along with her.

"Try them, until you know," he smiled.

She was only two turns away now. "Okay, answer my first question, please. Why do you keep doing this year after year, if no one listens?"

He paused in his tracks and gave her a genuine smile. "Because someday, I knew you'd come along," he said. Noor smiled at him and then stepped into the room. The old man stood outside. He waited, and waited. He hadn't been this nervous in decades. He waited to see young Noor's fate, and the fate of the world that she would change.

Moments later, Noor came out, and upon seeing her the old man fell to his knees in tears of happiness. For the young woman he saw in front of him, the beautiful angelic blossom he saw, had every color ever known to mankind on her, and a good number of colors never seen before.

I. Ashmawey

4

Fearing Below

I. Ashmawey

They told him a religious man is not afraid. Both parents, on many different occasions, separately and together, ingrained that law into his young, clay mind.
A religious man is not afraid.

That created a tremendous problem for six-year-old Alan, however. After all,
he felt like he had nothing but fear. And he, of course, wanted to be religious. He
was! He was religious. Just like his parents, but perhaps not as much. He'd never
reach their level but he'd never stop trying.

So he lay in bed early one morning, thinking of his failures from the day before. The birds chirped outside as the sun began to rise over cool, winter air. Laying
in his bed, eyes wide open, he listened to his grandma's snores as she slept next to
him. He distracted his thoughts by imagining she was a bear. With every snore, he
imagined a gigantic brown bear standing on it's hind legs, arms spread apart, snout
in the air letting out a tremendous growl. Alan got so scared from his own imagination that he had stop. He even had to sit up and look over his grandma's huge body,
sleeping on her side, just to see her face and make sure she didn't actually turn into
a bear. Once again, he had scared himself.

But a religious man is not afraid. And he was religious. And he was a man.
He returned to laying on his back. How was he to deal with yesterday's failure? He
had embarrassed himself in front of his parents, his grandma, his older siblings, and
probably half the town by the rate his mom spoke to others. Today, he would try
again. But... what would be the difference? He tried his absolute best yesterday and
failed miserably. And absolutely nothing had changed, yet he'd be trying again. Why?
Well, in reality he knew why. He knew he'd have to try again because his parents
would force him to. It wasn't like he had a choice in the matter. Especially given how
upset they were with him the day before.

Okay, if he was going to do this, may as well do it now. Get it over with. He
climbed down from the bed, careful not to wake grandma. He peaked from behind
the window blinds of his bedroom, careful not to bring in too much light, and
smiled at the blue jay sitting comfortably on the tree limb outside.

"Hi, Buster!" he whispered to the bird. Such a cute bird. He tiptoed out of the small, cramped room, trying to time each step with a snore to cover the sound of the creaking floor beneath him. Step, step, step, all the way to the door. As he exited the room in peace, he reminded himself, a religious man is not afraid. As young Alan moved swiftly like a blue jay, he was downstairs on the first floor of the old, decrepit wood house within seconds. With every step he took, he reminded himself why he was doing this. If he was to be a religious man, if he was to be loved by God, if he was ever going to enter the Kingdom of Heaven and escape the fires of Hell, he had to do this. For if he gave in to his fear, if he allowed himself to be scared, he wouldn't be religious. He knew God was watching him from above—looking down, waiting to see if he was going to be scared or not.

His steps got shorter, and slower. Maybe if he walked slow enough, something would happen and he wouldn't have to do it. His parents would wake up, or someone would knock on the door, or a tornado would hit and pick his house up carrying it all the way to Oz. All were possible, and all would save him from what he had to do next. But none of those happened. And no matter how slowly he crept across the wooden floor, he eventually reached the accursed door. There was no going back now. He switched on all the lights in sight and stared at the brass doorknob a good amount of time before reaching for it, slowly turning it, and ever so slowly opening the door. The creaking sound could be heard around the world.

It was just a basement.

That's all it was, just a basement. Why was he scared? Well, come on now. It wasn't the basement that scared him, no sir. No one is scared of a few walls, a floor, and a ceiling. It was what lurked in the basement, obviously. He knew there were creatures and spirits and he knew they were real, his parents had told him about them. They were terrifying, dark spirits that had the power to shape-shift, attack, and worst of all… possess you. He knew it all to be true, his parents had given him full accounts of these things happening to people they knew. The spirits were real. Yet, he could not be scared. Not now. Alan switched on the light at the top of the staircase.

"A religious man is not afraid," Alan said out loud to himself. He still had difficulty pronouncing R's, so they came out W's. He heard noises coming from the darkness at the bottom of the stairs because of course, his parents never cared to change the light bulb. Why would they? Alan closed his eyes, and listened. He squeezed his eyes shut really tight, because that would make him hear better. There was a hum, a constant, general, low hum in the basement. What was that? Alan knew, it must be a spirit. The hum grew louder. But even at six, Alan knew it must be something else. Something he didn't understand about basements. Something unnatural. Something about something. The point was, there was no way there was an actual spirit in his basement except… wait.

Alan saw a hint of a shadow move across the stairs. It appeared for a few seconds, climbing up the bottom few steps, then disappeared. There was no doubt in Alan's mind now, there were spirits, at least three, living in his basement. He began trembling with fear. His lips were shaking so fast he couldn't even utter the words out loud. "A religious… man… is not…. " And with that, he slammed the door shut and ran up the second story stairs. With every step, a scream louder than the one before. He jumped into bed, causing his grandma to almost get a heart attack. Both his parents ran into his bedroom with shocked eyes and palpitating hearts.

"What's wrong?! What happened?!" they screamed at him. He was terrified, and couldn't explain a thing. He wasn't scared of the spirits, for those lived in the basement. He wasn't scared of the basement, for he was now upstairs.

Shaking in his bed, hiding under the covers, he repeated one sentence over and over.

"I'm not a religious man. I'm not a religious man. I'm not a religious man." And the problem was, the real problem was, that he knew what that meant. And he knew where he'd go after he died.

I. Ashmawey

5

The Laughing Stock

I. Ashmawey

They laugh.

They laugh and laugh and laugh to their heart's content. So much so that they lift their faces to the ceiling above to catch their breath. Tears fall from the corners of their eyes as they wipe and slobber. They don't want to take their eyes off the TV but can't keep their eyes on it any longer either, they're barely able to breathe! And it is just too funny, just too darn funny.

So the four of them sit there, the Father, the Mother, the Son, and the Daughter. Sitting together—bodies touching on the crowded loveseat but entirely alone—pointing and laughing. And pointing and laughing. The colors on their faces change as the flashing lights from the TV show the hilariousness of life. Their laughter is heard echoing in the neighborhood. It clashes with similar laughter coming from every small home down the dark street, all watching the same program.

It's the donut, you see. The donut makes everything all the more hilarious. The pudgy policeman on the TV is so intimately enjoying his pink glazed donut with too many sprinkles. Sitting in his police car with the windows up, he closes his eyes with every loving bite. Belly resting on his steering wheel and shirt buttons barely closing, his radio playing jolly Christmasy tunes.

The family laughs.

Outside the policeman's car, an old man is being robbed. A burglar holds him up at gunpoint, and ravages the old man's wallet and all his possessions. Why the burglar thinks it's a good idea to rob somebody right next to a police car, no one knows. And no one cares. The old man yells and screams at the top of his lungs. But no one is there, save the hungry policeman. He can't hear the screams over his loud music. The old man's face turns blue with screaming. And as the policeman finishes his last bite, just as he licks his fingers clean of the frosting, just as he picks the fallen sprinkles off his belly and throws them in his mouth… he pulls out another donut. Maple glazed.

The family laughs. Goodness, they can't get enough of this guy.

The burglar shoots the old man whose body then hits the passenger side of the police car and falls to the ground. The burglar stuffs his hands in the dead man's jacket pockets then runs off. The policeman finally notices. Shocked at what he sees, he stuffs the rest of his second donut into his mouth and hurries out of the car.

The entire street of houses roars with laughter as the policeman waddles around the dead body, pulling up his falling pants and tucking in his shirt.

The policeman looks over the dead body. If only he had gotten to him in time! He takes off his cap and scratches his head. Now what? Well, he's going to have to call backup. That's the only thing he could do, really. He's going to call backup. But, wait. Wait a minute. What's that the dead old man is holding? A bag? A paper bag. Wonder what's inside it. The policeman decides to bend down just for a peek. He peers inside it, and what do you know? He pulls out a donut. Chocolate!

"Well," the policeman says to the dead man. "I don't suspect you'll be wanting this." He stuffs it in his mouth. The family loses their marbles. The Son falls off the couch in laughter. The Mother snorts louder than a pig, she can't catch her breath. The Sister then laughs at the Mother's snorting.

The Father though, his laugh is the strongest. It's so strong it never comes out. The Father has a heart attack right then and there. It was that chocolate donut, it put him over the edge. It was just too funny. He falls over, dead. The Son is the first to notice. Continuing to laugh, he points at his Father.

"Daddy's dead! He laughed too hard!" he points. The three of them roar with more laughter at that. That someone would die from laughing, it's hilarious! Oh, at least he died happy.

On the TV, the policeman sits down next to the dead body, as the family sits next to theirs. The policeman is stuffed now, three donuts in his probably already full belly. He has to lie down a bit. He uses the old man's stomach as a pillow and rests his head as he sleeps on his back. The old man's blood trails away from his body down the sidewalk pavement.

The house is now in full shaking from the laughter. The entire street is.

Then, darkness. A cold, silent darkness. The power is out. It's out on the entire street. The family of now three looks to each other.

"Mother," the Daughter says, "what do we do?"

"I don't…I don't know!" she screams. "It's all just so horrible and annoying. How could it just stop working all of a sudden? Who has power outages in this day and age?!" She is furious. So much so, that she cries.

She cries and weeps and whines. Her children cry with her. The whole street cries from agony. For they could no longer live.

6

The Next Stage of Evolution

I. Ashmawey

*O*n *Earth...*
His name was Ali. A young and imaginative six-year-old boy who loved nothing more than playing with Legos. Building things, that's what made most sense to Ali. From a young age, he exhibited unique forms of intelligence most people many years his senior struggled to understand. And because his strengths weren't understood by most, often times they would go unnoticed. For example, Ali had a difficult time finding interest in his surroundings. This was because he had too much going on in his own mind. The deepest oceans of his consciousness gave him ample material to explore for many lifetimes over.

Sitting on his family room carpet with his black, curly hair growing too long, he would imagine and build Lego worlds for hours. Building, and building, and building! His hands couldn't move fast enough for his creativity. And then after every Lego was used, there was always the inevitable sad moment of demolishing his creations. He understood that if he was ever to live the happy times of creating once again, he would first have to destroy. Unlike other boys his age who enjoyed demolition, he hated it.

Ali wanted to create.

It was an inherent desire in every human, wasn't it? To make something where there was nothing before? To leave a footprint after you've gone to say *I was here!*

And what a day to conceive! How perfectly timely for young Ali to continue his love for creating, for it was a special day. To date, it was the greatest day in the history of human evolution. All TVs, smartphones, tablets, smartglasses, smartwatches, smartwalls, and smarthomes were watching the same thing. United, a monumental juncture for humanity. Evolved beings—after having set aside their differences, after having moved past the petty wars and fighting—finally decide to come together to explore new worlds. It wasn't easy; it took millennia of battling that almost led to complete annihilation. But thankfully, they managed to pull through it. And instead of extinction, humanity was now ready for the next stage of their evolution.

And so it was in this one particular, small, modest home, on this one quiet, average street in the middle of America, that something beautiful happened. As Ali played, his happy, thirty-year-old parents put their smartglasses on. Looking at their smartwalls, they received the full 360 experience of what the entire world was observing: the first city being built on Mars. Sure, humans had already inhabited the moon. But the moon was ours, in our backyard, so to speak. So the accomplishment there felt smaller. But Mars! The red planet of saffron dirt and silver rivers. There was no questioning how immense of an occurrence it was.

Ali's father sat on the couch next to his wife, carrying her hand in his. They watched the building machine, a huge apparatus controlled by a Chief Engineer, ride out to the predetermined coordinates in the new city of Macedonia on Mars. And with the push of a button, the building machine was set in motion. Immediately, rock formations were pounded to dust and holes were dug in their stead. Foundations were placed, enormous beams buried into the Martian dirt. And within two minutes, the first man-made building was erected on Mars.

The smile on the mother's face stretched across the galaxy, reaching all 141 million miles to Mars. Next to her, a single tear formed at the corner of the father's eye and rolled down his cheek. A tear that carried all the happiness of a hard working generation. A generation that dreamt, imagined, pursued, and achieved.

What a feat.

What a day.

They prepared for the next building, as there would be more for sure. The couple did not know exactly how many buildings would be built or what they would look like as the plans weren't public knowledge. But that made the observing all the more exciting, didn't it!?

Ali's father wanted to take off his smartglasses to look back at his son, to see what he was so occupied with. He wished so much that he could share this amazing moment with him. But alas, Ali was far too young to understand the relevance of such an event. Or, perhaps Ali's father simply didn't want to take the smartglasses off, so he convinced himself his son wouldn't understand. After all, to miss a second of this moment would have been such a shame.

But behind the couch, and in the dark, young Ali continued building with his Legos. He had one structure completed. Beautiful, standing like a castle with four peaks, one on each corner. A content smile sat on Ali's face. Eyes glowing, he turned the structure around and examined it from the other side. Perfect. A job well done. He had created a plan for his structure and he had executed it perfectly. A wonderful sense of accomplishment came over him.

On the smartwalls and smartglasses, and all across the world, people admired the first structure on Mars. It was a classical building that resembled a castle, with four peaks, one on each corner.

Ali moved on to the next structure, as did the men on Mars. Ali's second structure was smaller, a few steps away from one of the corners of the first building. Long and singular, this structure resembled a lighthouse or a standalone minaret. For Ali, this was easy. He simply stacked up layers of Legos making a rectangular cuboid.

On the couch, Ali's parents watched the second structure rise on Mars, a singular minaret a few hundred yards away from one of the corners of the first structure. It would appear Ali was an excellent mimicker. Not unusual for his age but still impressive.

And even though Ali knew exactly what he wanted to do next, he didn't move onto it immediately. Not yet. First, he had to perfect what he had. He wanted to make sure there was a direct invisible line between the corner of the first structure and a corner of the second building dissecting both exactly at forty-five degrees. Perfection yields excellence, a law the young boy lived by even with his toys. Especially with his toys. As to him, they were everything.

When Ali was building, he didn't see his creations as momentary existences made of Legos. Rather, Ali saw them rising from the ground, going through the clouds, and reaching up into the heavens. He saw masses of people beholding them, gazing upon them with adoration. He saw people using them, inhabiting them, calling them home. Children playing in the yards out front, neighbors getting to know each other across the halls, going up and down the elevators. The doorman bidding people farewell every morning, wishing them wonderful days, and welcoming back home them each evening. Decorating the lobby with a beautiful Christmas tree during the holidays. The buildings were alive. In every essence of the word, they were alive.

Ali saw the buildings, and so they became real.

On Mars...

A Systems Engineer sitting inside the Engineering Booth sent a call to the Chief Engineer operating the building machine. The machine was similar to a massive tractor but with a much larger control deck, fully encapsulated and atmosphere altered.

"Sir, I'm getting calls from NASA. They're asking why you're not following the plans," he asked.

"What do you mean?" the Chief Engineer cried out. He put down his controls that resembled virtual reality video game controllers and looked out the window of his control deck. He peered over to the Engineering Booth to make eye contact with the Systems Engineer. "I am following the plans!"

"Sir, they're saying that you've entirely deviated from the plans that they are sending." The Systems Engineer was surrounded by a plethora of confused engineers, all looking at each other questioningly. Why was the Chief Engineer not following the plans? Did he have a hidden agenda? Was there something he knew that they didn't? It was difficult to question him of course, given his high position. But something had to be said!

"I have the plans right here! They're being fed into receiver!" the Chief Engineer screamed in frustration. His voice was loud and full of confidence. "How could I possibly deviate? The building machine wouldn't let me even if I tried!"

"I don't know sir," the Systems Engineer said with reluctance in his voice. "I just... they're saying you're deviating."

There was a long pause. The Chief Engineer's face scrunched. His mouth hung open for a second. "If they're not sending me these plans, who is?"

Back on Earth...

Ali stared at his completed city. A monumental, main building in the center and four minarets beyond each corner. People would love his buildings. People would use them and be happy with them forever.

His parents still sat on the couch, watching and observing. Seeing the amazing feats of humanity. They sat there, eyes covered by the smartglasses, minds engulfed in the smartwalls, completely unaware that the greatest step in human evolution was taking place right behind their couch.

7

A Room with a Table

I. Ashmawey

They sat at an old, wooden table—three chairs, roughly equidistant from each other—in a room with four walls and a door. The walls were covered by a deep burgundy wallpaper with a patterned Fleur-de-lis of a similarly colored velvet, running in columns up and down the walls. Completing the film noir setting, a single, antique, brass chandelier hung above the elaborate, cherry table.

It wasn't the room that was important however, nor the table, it was who sat at the table. Let's meet them. Booker was the first to speak.

"I'm gonna go out on a limb here," Booker said in a low voice, "and assume you all just opened our eyes now. And that the two of you have no idea how you got here either." To his right, a young lady with long blonde hair nodded her head. Her mouth hung open and her eyes close to tears. To his left, a similarly aged man in his thirties, bald and slightly overweight, sat with furrowed eyebrows looking down at the table. He was huffing beneath his breath. "I'm also assuming the last thing the two of you remember is eating at the Italian joint on Bleecker and Mercer." The two nodded again. "Okay. Let's start with the etiquette. My name is Booker. I'm thirty-three."

A bit of a pause.

"I'm—" the blonde said in a broken voice. She cleared her throat. "I'm Laurel. Thirty-three." Booker nodded at her. She looked younger to him. They both looked to the other guy, whose eyebrows became stern.

"Hank," he said in a deep voice.

"Of course you are. Same age?" Booker asked. Hank nodded. "Okay…" he paused. "Okay. Let's rule things out, shall we?"

"Is this real?" Laurel asked. She looked all around her, at the walls and the ceiling. She lifted her left hand and touched it with her right, squeezing the skin on her knuckles.

Booker rolled his eyes. "Laurel, is it?" She nodded. "Laurel, yes, the first thing is usually to check if this is real or not. Is it a dream? Is it all in our heads, like some Matrix thing? That's typical. But there's a limit to how much you can trust movies. The reality is, a dream always feels different than real life, right? You can

49

always tell. And the question about it being in our heads, well, I don't think technology has gotten that far yet. So, while we *should* be ruling things out, this one's a given, I think." Laurel nodded her head very quickly in agreement. She was taking very short breaths as she darted her eyes from wall to wall to ceiling to wall. "Take deep breaths, Laurel. We'll be okay."

"You... talk... way too much," Hank growled, still staring at the table in anger.

"I'd like to get us out of here, Hank," Booker responded curtly. "If that's okay with you, of course."

"I don't know you. Either of you. This could be all a set up by the two of you," Hank said, finally lifting his eyes to scowl at the two.

"You're skipping a few steps here, but okay." Booker got up from his seat. He quickly grabbed at the table, catching his balance. Clearly, his legs weren't working to their full capacity. He pushed himself back up. Booker was the fit, athletic type. His brown hair perfectly styled and combed to the side. "Let's talk about all the possibilities here."

"And how would you know the possibilities if you aren't behind this?" Hank asked, voice elevating.

"Hank, this isn't new. I watch movies by the boatload. People, locked in a room, not knowing each other. We've seen it a million times. It's never creative, it's never new. And it's always the same possibilities. Okay?"

"He's right," Laurel said. She finally sounded sure of herself for once. "I've seen it before, a number of times actually. And I don't even watch much TV."

"There you go. So, the viable possibilities, ignoring of course whether or not this is real. Let's go through them." Booker finally felt the blood rush through his legs again. He began pacing around the table but incredibly slowly. "The way I see it, there are three options. Either this is set up by one of us, possibly two of us. That's option one. Option two, a third party is holding us for some sadistic reason. To see if we hurt each other. Or maybe for observation, could be aliens."

"Aliens. But this being in our heads isn't a viable option?" Hank sneered.

"Option three," Booker said. "This is a prank. We're on some TV show right now and after a few minutes, some C-list Hollywood dropout will come waltzing in with cameras."

That made Laurel smile. "I think it's that option," she said.

"No, you hope it's that option," Hank snapped. "I think it's what I've felt all along." He slowly got up from the table. And just like Booker, he had a difficult time regaining use of his legs. "Well, I take that back. I thought for a moment it was both of you that were in on it. But she doesn't strike me as the type. I think it's you, Booker. Whatever the hell kind of name that is."

"Of course you do. Would you mind telling me why you think I'd be doing this?" Booker asked with his arms resting on his hips. Laurel played ping pong with her pupils between them.

"You're the one that watches the movies. You tell me why the sick-minded villains do this kind of thing. It's usually entertainment, isn't it?" Hank asked.

"Sure, it's entertainment because they're sadistic freaks. Is that how I strike you?"

"What the hell would I know?!" Hank screamed. "I just met you!"

"Okay!" Laurel yelled. She took a deep breath, regaining her composure. "Okay. You don't know him, Hank. You admitted it yourself."

"So?"

"So how about you do? Sit down, both of you. Please," she said calmly. The two men looked to each other and locked eyes. Booker felt like he was in an old western standoff. At any moment, a tumbleweed would come rolling between them. Eventually, they both complied with Laurel's request. "Thank you both. I mean it, thank you. You didn't have to listen to me but it means a lot to me that you did." Booker smiled at her. Hank nodded with his eyes closed. "Okay, I'd like us each to say something about ourselves."

"I don't trust either of you to say anything," Hank said quickly.

"Same here, pal," Booker bickered.

"That's fine!" Laurel stopped them. "That's fine. Nothing identifying. Not even your occupations. How about just something you enjoy. No harm in that, right?" Both men shrugged. "I'll assume that means you both agree. Great. I'll start. Something I enjoy: reading. I love books. I devour them. Every morning, every night, and a lot in between. My favorites are the old books. Verne. Shaw. Doyle. Baum. They arouse emotions in me that I can't get anywhere else." Neither of the men commented or said anything. "How about you, Booker?"

He took a deep breath, thinking hard about what to say. "Okay, fine. Movies. I love watching movies."

"What kind?" Laurel asked.

"All of them. Horror. Drama. Action. Thriller. Comedies. Even the Rom-Coms," he threw in.

"Do you like the older stuff better or the new?" she asked.

"Same. I like both. I think that's enough sharing for me," he said curtly.

"Okay, Hank. What about you?" Laurel asked.

"Fine," Hank said, rather abruptly. It's not like he didn't know it was coming. "I watch sports. And before you ask which ones, football, baseball, and hockey. Too much action in basketball, not enough skill. Golf bores the hell out of me. Anyone who watches that is wasting his life almost as much as those who play it. Soccer isn't a sport, you're just running ninety percent of the time."

"Wow, so charming this guy," Booker commented.

"He didn't judge your movie-watching, or my book-reading," Laurel said.

"Okay, that was nice and all. Laurel, that was nice," Booker said. "But I don't know you guys any better and I don't know whether or not any of you two could have done this. I'm going to ask you each a question, and this one's personal."

"That goes both ways, buddy," Hank chimed in.

"Fine," Booker responded. "Each of us names a personal goal. And the other two will be able to tell if it's genuine or not. If it isn't genuine, then you're lying. If you're lying, then that means you have another goal. Something occupying your mind at the moment, which means that you're probably behind this."

"Idiotic thought process, but I'm game," Hank said.

"Me too," Laurel said.

"Great," Booker began. "I'll start. My goal is to become a movie critic. I watch movies day and night. Why not get paid for it?"

"I like that goal, it uses what you love," Laurel commented. "Why haven't you done it yet?"

Booker shrugged his shoulders. "You know how it is. It's not easy starting something like that, ya know? I mean, I guess I could start a blog, or apply for one of the newspapers or something. Anyway, enough about me. You go, Laurel."

"Okay, my goal is to be a published author," she said.

"Alright. When do you plan on doing that?" Booker asked.

"I wrote a novel. I had it professionally edited. And now I'm going through it again," she responded.

"So what's stopping you from trying to get it published?" Hank asked. Laurel froze. Her mouth open, and her eyes like ice. "Say the truth. We're judging you," Hank added.

"I'm scared… of rejection," she responded. There was an awkward pause, a silence, as Laurel looked down to the table.

"Alright, I want to play hockey. That's my freaking goal," Hank said, angry at the world.

"And why don't you? You have the perfect attitude," Booker joked.

"Do you not see my gut? It's pretty obvious," Hank scoffed.

"So get rid of it," Booker said.

"Before being here, I was at an Italian restaurant ordering a pizza and a tagliatelle pasta for myself. Yeah, I'll lose the gut. You just wait," Hank said.

"Of course you will," Laurel said, with no sarcasm in her voice whatsoever. "You will. You want it, and so you will." She locked eyes with Hank. She was so sincere that it scared him. He looked away.

"Okay, so there we are. Our goals. Now what?" Hank asked.

Just then, the door opened. Four paramedics walked in with a roller bed. Two men, and two women. The woman in the lead spoke.

"Are you three okay?"

"What the goddamn hell?" Hank screamed.

"Relax," the paramedic said, while her three colleagues walked over calmly to the three at the table and took their vitals. "Do you not… do you not remember what happened?"

"No, obviously we don't," Booker said.

"Yeah, that makes sense actually. The gas could have temporary amnesiac tendencies. There was a pretty major gas leak in the restaurant," the paramedic explained. "A lot of people passed out. We've been treating all the patients and we were crowding the streets. We took a few of you to this back room to escape the gas until it was all vacuumed."

"Then why'd you lock us in here?" Laurel asked.

The paramedic looked at her, confused. She looked back at the door behind her which they came in from. "You weren't locked in."

"Are you saying the door was open? All we had to do was get up and go through?" Booker asked.

"Yes," the paramedic said, still confused. "That's how doors work," she laughed. "Wanting to get out doesn't usually work on its own. You have to open them and go through."

The three looked to each other. Had they just shut up and gone through the door, they would have all been much happier. Had they not assumed it would be locked, and impossible to go through. Had they at least tried to achieve what they wanted.

Had they just done that…

I. Ashmawey

8

The King's Tablet

I. Ashmawey

E dison clutched his carry-on bag tight to his chest. All five hours from Orange County to New York, then another twelve hours from New York to Cairo, Egypt, and the carry-on did not leave the vicinity of his heart, suffocated by his arms. He checked his trusty manual Omega Speedmaster, they'd be landing any minute. Twenty year old Edison was old-fashioned like that; watches, printed books, conversations with real human beings, he wasn't into technology. While everyone on the plane around him was engulfed into their screens, Edison lifted the window cover and looked out onto the wide, sandy desert.

In the furthest distance of the silky yellow horizon, he noticed the three immortal friends who have stood the test of time. To call the Pyramids 'Great' was a shameful understatement. He felt such a tremendous closeness to these colossal structures, particularly given what he held in his carry-on. He squeezed it even tighter, feeling that all those around him on the flight might accidentally discover the secret he held. None of them did, but paranoia could convince one of anything, can't it?

You see, Edison's father was one of the most famous Egyptologists in the field. In his last excavation, an accident occurred that resulted in the death of the acclaimed scientist and historian. This was ten years ago, Edison was but a young lad then. Years later, his late father's best friend came to visit him, a man he hadn't seen since his father's funeral. He gave Edison a small wooden box and told him that before his father had been murdered inside the pyramid, he had found something: a tablet that belonged to King Khnum-Khufu. He was able to sneak the tablet out before he was killed. This of course came as a shock to young Edison. Not the tablet, but the fact that his father was allegedly murdered, as he had always believed it was an accident. Who would have killed his father in the middle of an expedition? And why?

As it were, briefly after this encounter and Edison receiving the tablet, his father's friend was killed in a car accident. A car accident? Edison knew better. The tablet was important. It had something crucial, and Edison would find out what it was.

I. Ashmawey

And so at the ripe age of twenty with a Master's degree in Egyptology hanging above his desk at home, Edison was on a quest to complete whatever his father was not able to. He tore open the small bag of peanuts and poured them onto the airplane tray in front of him. Seven peanuts, why were they always an odd number? He ran his fingers through his long brown hair that reached the nape of his neck and rested his head back.

He closed his eyes.

He needed to think about the words left by King Khufu. It had taken him years to correctly translate them. And when he did, he learned the tablet was actually a key. A map for something far greater than any ancient Egyptian discovery made before.

Some know not one another. Not recognize neighbor's faces. Some forget even themselves. The cure for the illness is buried with me. So that our sons may use it.
-- King Khnum-Khufu

After years of research, months of analysis, studying and restudying and reviewing every facet of ancient Egyptian history, Edison finally understood the tablet. He knew the ancient Egyptians were advanced in medical science, astronomy, geometry, and other fields. But this tablet could only mean one thing.

Not recognizing neighbor's faces…

Some forgetting even themselves…

The ancient Egyptians had found a cure for Alzheimer's. And the cure was buried with the King himself. Edison knew the sarcophagus had been emptied many centuries ago by grave robbers. But according to the tablet and to Edison's research, the cure was hidden beneath the sarcophagus. Once modern scientists first excavated the pyramid and saw that the burial place was empty, disappointed, they looked no further. Nobody ever thought to look beneath. It was so simple, yet so brilliant.

Two days later, and after many sandy hours traveling on the back of a camel that enjoyed the taste of Levi's jeans, Edison arrived at the footsteps of the greatest of the Great Pyramids. His eyes had been down the entire camel ride due to the flying sand. Even with his face wrapped in a traditional scarf and thick-framed Oakley's, there were still little bullying packets of sand finding their way into his corneas. How do desert dwellers live like this? Was the desert this harsh in ancient times?

His pondering was cut short as his camel was abruptly stopped. At first he was hesitant to raise his eyes back into the blowing sand, but a beautiful voice finally made him look up.

"Edison Telfort?" an accented, feminine voice asked. A short, thin, young woman with straight black hair and sandy tan skin stood under his camel. She caressed the camel's face while smiling at Edison. "Welcome to Cairo."

"Thank you. You must be Hend," he said. She nodded in return. They had communicated by phone a few times, she would be his guide. A small inkling of a smile grew on her face. She liked him. He looked unkempt, and something about him struck her as traditional. Perhaps it was his coke-bottle glasses when others would have opted for laser eye surgery. Or maybe it was his retro sweater tied around his waist. Or possibly his manual wristwatch in a world of digital screens.

A few moments later, the two plunged into a balmy bath of dampness as they stepped into the pyramid. The air's warmth found its way into their nostrils and quickly filled up their lungs. To Edison, it was like being hit by a parade of water bullets in his chest. He gasped for oxygen and fell to the ground in the process. Hend chuckled at the sight of him.

"You will get used to it, Edison," she smiled. "Catch your breath. We have hours before we reach the tomb." And hours was correct. Edison never did get used to the thickness of the air, it was like swimming in a lake with no reprieve. And to make matters worse, the first hour of their trek was in a pathway with a three-foot-high ceiling. It was an annoying height where Edison couldn't decide whether to crawl on his knees or just profoundly bend his back. Hend though, she slithered her way through like a pro. Edison liked that she used a torch and not a flashlight. Something about that was refreshing to him.

"You haven't taken out your camera once. No pictures at all," she mentioned to him as she continued to lead the way.

"Yeah, I uh…" Edison struggled to keep up. "I prefer to experience things rather than see them behind a lens."

This made Hend smile. "So what do you plan on doing with the cure when you find it?" she asked as they continued crawling.

"Save people," Edison responded immediately. Not an ounce of ingenuity was heard in his voice. "Alzheimer's, dementia, it's… I mean, I know it's not usually fatal. But it certainly affects lives."

"It does. But of course, you will make much money."

"I'm not going to sell it," he responded. "Our world is bad enough," he explained. "People don't care about each other. If I can do something to help fix that, anything at all, then I will."

Hend smiled to herself. "Good."

Hours later, they finally reached the room which held the sacred tomb. Edison felt such a relief finally being able to stand upright. His back let out a loud crack the moment he straightened it. He and Hend got right to work, digging beneath where the sarcophagus once lay. It was roughly half an hour later when they unearthed a large chest, maybe three feet wide. It was made of clay and bore the King's emblem on the side.

"This is it!" Edison screamed. Suddenly he got a tremendous rush of energy.

Within minutes, they had both completed unearthed it.

Opening the lid, they both froze in confusion. "This must be a mistake," he said. He reached inside the chest... and pulled out a cell phone! Not any brand he recognized, but definitely a cell phone made of plastic. He looked it over closely, it looked ancient. But at the same time, looked like it was manufactured yesterday.

"Look at this," Hend called. She had pulled out a small television and a cassette tape, all coming from inside the chest. What on Earth was going on?

Then Edison found something strange. It was a small black gadget shaped like a box, not more than three inches to a side. On one of the sides was a prominent red button. He held up the box and examined it closely. It had a few symbols engraved on the bottom. Because of all the research he had done, he knew the symbols easily.

"This will spread the cure," Edison read.

"Edison, I don't understand anything," Hend said.

"I think I do. Hend, what if the disease King Khufu spoke of wasn't Alzheimer's? What if the ancient Egyptians battled a completely different kind of illness?"

"What illness? What else could lead to people not knowing their neighbors or even knowing who they themselves are?" Hend asked, confused.

"I think I know." And with that, Edison hit the red button.

And in one second, in one quick flash, every electronic device on the face of the planet went dead. Never to turn on again.

9

Two Brothers on their Way

I. Ashmawey

The date was February 18, 1863. The sixtieth birthday of our mother, Sarah Paulton. Due to the celebration, my brothers, Alexander and Harrison, temporarily ended their quarreling. They sat on opposite ends of the dinner table; one wore blue, and one wore gray. They did not end the quarrel by choice, mind you. It was Father's anger that convinced them. He was mighty enraged at them for causing so much commotion on such an important day. It was for the best anyway— on that day, both Alexander and Harrison surely realized they would never agree. Even I, while being many years younger than them both, knew this to be fact very early on. Sometimes it is best when you realize you will not agree with someone, to cease the discussion as early as possible.

That day was one of their longest arguments and certainly one of their most heated. It began with Alexander this time. During Mother's birthday dinner, he mentioned to Father he was inquiring about purchasing a slave for our uncle who lived in Alabama. Harrison was so incredibly offended by the topic, for he knew that Alexander was trying to get a rise out of him.

"Just saying those words, Alexander," Harrison said, "do you not feel filthy in your chest?"

"How does your duck taste, brother?" Alexander asked. Harrison was bewildered by the question, as I and our parents were as well.

"My duck?" Harrison asked. "My duck is fine, Alexander. Do not sway from the topic."

"Do you not feel it unjust for you to kill a poor duck and feed upon its flesh?" Alexander asked. Father cleared his throat upon hearing this, hinting to Alexander that the question was not appropriate. Mother pretended not to hear it. She took a large bite out of her duck breast and continued on her meal.

"Preposterous," Harrison responded. "It is God's will. He created these animals for us to feed. He created the world for us!"

"I happen to agree," Alexander said. "The world was in fact created for us. And in it, a natural order. What differs then when I tell you that as cows were created to provide us milk, and chickens created to provide us eggs, and bees created to provide us honey, so too were slaves created to provide us comfort? Why is this so difficult to understand?!"

"The difference is that slaves are humans," Harrison bellowed.

"Yes, God created them in our same shape so that they may better serve us," Alexander added curtly.

"What if He did not?" Harrison asked.

"Harrison…" Father chimed in, finally. But that was all he had to add, in fact. Mother still continued with her duck. I continued darting my eyes between my two brothers like a game of badminton.

"What do you mean? Of course, He did," Alexander responded.

"I mean, what if He did not create them to serve us? What if He created them to be our equals?" Harrison asked.

"That is a very compelling question," I added; rather obnoxiously, I admit.

"Hush, Petunia," Mother finally spoke. I was too young to engage in these conversations.

"It is, in fact, an interesting notion, brother," Alexander responded. "But then why did the good Lord create them to look so incredibly different from us? Does that not imply that they are, in fact, different? And that therefore, they are not the same as us?"

"Funny, you were just arguing they look the same as us. But very well, no matter. We look different and therefore we must be different. What if God created us to serve them, then?" Harrison asked with a smile.

"Harrison!" Mother screamed. "How unseemly. How dare you speak like this?"

"Why do you wish to be preposterous? It really does not serve for good conversation," Alexander said with an air of ego.

"I wish to only serve a point. And that is… how would we know? There are hundreds of colors of birds. Does that necessarily mean that one bird was created to serve another? How about cows? The black, the white, the brown?"

"You're missing a very important point, Harrison. The cows look different. But none of them enslaved the other, because they cannot. The fact that we have enslaved them, and have been doing so for years, and they have not resisted, is proof enough that this is the natural order of things."

"They have not resisted only because our weapons are stronger than theirs," Harrison responded through his teeth.

"Well then, there you have it. We are more superior. You said it yourself," Alexander said, with the same guile.

"In weaponry, yes. Too bad, not in humanity. Seems we lost all that and became like the animals," Harrison added.

"Okay, that's enough! Both of you!" Father said standing up firmly. "Look here! Look!" Father pointed at Mother who had her head down and a handkerchief up to her mouth. "Look how strongly you have both upset your mother. And for what?!" Father took a deep breath before whispering something only audible to himself. "Listen, you two. You are both here for one night and one night only. And then you head off again to fight your wretched war. At the very least, let us have a decent meal. God help us all."

And with that, Harrison and Alexander did not speak again. For the remainder of the evening, it was as though the two did not see each other. Not one acknowledgment passed between them.

After dinner we enjoyed Mother's birthday cake, chocolate with pecan and caramel. And still not a word between my brothers. After the cake and tea, Father took both my brothers into his study. Thankfully, I had discovered years ago that my bedroom fireplace shares a chimney with the study below.

"Boys," Father began. "No, you're no longer boys, are you?" Father paused a moment. He was deep in thought, I could tell. "My Lord, my sons are now men. But it does not change that they quarrel. Harrison, you must recognize that this war is tearing the country apart. It's tearing apart homes, families, brothers! What if there is a natural order of things? What if that natural order is being disturbed?"

"We've read the good book many a times, Father. He speaks of all He has given us. Do you feel He neglected to mention that He created a race of humans for our pleasure? To enslave and burden?" Harrison responded. There was a short quiet after that.

"No. No, God does not neglect," Father said. "Perhaps... it is possible that we have been doing wrong. Perhaps, the natural order of things was not in fact so natural. Perhaps we have been doing things wrong. And when that is the case, it is not so easily changed."

And Father ended with that. My two brothers did not speak again. No one spoke again that night. They kissed Mother goodbye, they bid Father farewell, they hugged me goodnight... all separately. There was no more arguing that night.

It was for the best perhaps. Sometimes it is best, when you realize that you will not agree with someone, to cease the discussion as soon as possible. Unless of course, you replace the discussion with battle. I would have much rather Alexander and Harrison continue quarreling at home, and Mother's birthday be ruined, than witnessing what I witnessed a few weeks later, when one brother came home and the other stayed behind.

One brother came home, having murdered the other.

I. Ashmawey

10

Before the Beginning

I. Ashmawey

"And I think it's going to be a long, long time…" Apolena sang to herself. "Till touchdown brings me round again to find."

"Come in Crown," a voice over the loud speaker spoke.

"This is U.S.S. Crown responding," Apolena said.

"That's a heck of a singing voice you got there, Kip," the voice said with some sarcasm.

Apolena smiled to herself. "Thank you, sir. I've had some time to practice."

"You're approaching the point of no contact, Kip. Two hours out."

"Yes sir," she said. A long pause followed. They both had so much to say but said nothing at all. Sometimes silence speaks the loudest.

"You'll be fine, Apolena," the voice said. "You'll come back to us. A hero."

"An explorer, sir," she said quickly and curtly. "I'm sorry, I just… if I'm remembered as anything sir, please let it be an explorer. Not a hero."

"You got it, Kip. Houston out." And with that, she was alone again. Floating in a tin can, far above the world.

She looked at her navigation screen and magnified the view of Earth. So beautiful, so peaceful. Apolena Kip was attempting something never before attempted in the history of her species. For her entire lifetime, people have been traveling back and forth through much of the past. Never the future, but they've covered a plethora of eras from protohistory. Apolena Kip, however, she was on an incredibly special expedition 13.7 billion years into the past. This was a time particularly special, as it was the date of the big bang. And she was the first to travel that far back.

As far as scientific advancements had taken humans, scientists knew and were able to calculate everything that occurred in the universe starting a millionth of a second after the big bang, but not at zero hour. The moment right before the big bang, no one knew anything about what existence looked like. Why was that so important? Because all the rules and laws of physics, mathematics, and science that we have today made it *impossible* for the big bang to have ever occurred. So how did it happen? If the laws of the universe wouldn't have allowed for the big bang to happen, then what kind of laws existed before? Were there any laws before to begin with? And if there were, what happened to them? Why did those laws cease to exist from after the big bang? We didn't know. And that's why Apolena Kip was so important.

In her last few moments of contact with NASA, she did not choose to talk to her friends, her family, or her coworkers on earth; nobody. Rather, she chose to meditate. She put on Vivaldi's Spring and closed her eyes. She reclined back in her oversized chair in her tiny, one man vessel. The craft was nothing more than a control deck with hundreds of holographic buttons floating above a desk-like panel surrounding her chair, a small bed behind her, and an even smaller bathroom.

Ideally, Apolena would travel back 13.7 billion years, gather all the desired measurements and data, and travel forward again to the present. All parties involved, including Apolena, knew that this was a long shot, however. Since, if she was to observe the big bang, how could she possibly survive it? The measuring equipment on the outside of the vessel could survive, it was made of an incredibly strong alloy that was pressure tested to withstand the phenomena of the big bang. Even if the equipment itself was destroyed, the data would not. The same alloy could not be used for the vessel as it did not create an environment suitable for living. So there was no telling what would happen to the vessel or Apolena Kip. But if she didn't survive, at least the data would. And so, a few minutes after the big bang, there would be a colleague of hers from NASA who traveled back 13.7 billion years minus a few moments, waiting to retrieve the measuring equipment.

"Crown, this is Houston," the voice spoke again.

"U.S.S. Crown here," Apolena responded.

"Five minutes to point of no contact," the voice said. It was referring to the commencement of the time travel, after which point, the time traveler could no longer have contact with the present world.

"Yes sir," Apolena responded.

"As you've been trained, due to the tremendous timespan you will be traveling, the time travel will not be linear." For the first few minutes, she'd be traveling at ten years a minute. After roughly ten minutes, so 100 years back, her time travel speed would increase to 1000 years a minute. This speed would increase till it reaches 750 million years per minute. This acceleration could allow her to reach before the big bang in about fifteen minutes. However, that wasn't what was going to happen. NASA had planned it so that the vessel slowed down to close to a halt right after the big bang. Apolena would get a few minutes to observe the big bang, and then slowly travel to before it.

"I understand sir. I'm ready," Apolena said.

"I know you are. Sound out, please," the voice said.

"This is Apolena Kip, of Peoria, Illinois. Captain of the U.S.S. Crown. Twenty-seven years old. The date is two-thousand, one-hundred and two. I am attempting to travel back in time to moments before the big bang, roughly 13.7 billion years ago. I plan to return to the present. If I do not, the data I gather will," Apolena said in the most mechanical voice. "I hope this mission…" she took a deep breath. This was when a tear formed at the corner of her eye. She wiped it quickly before pushing back her long, brown hair. "I hope this mission inspires others. If nothing else, I hope it emboldens us to continue to explore. It is our nature to always look beyond the hill to the other side. And when we do, we find the next hill. A bigger hill. This here is the ultimate hill. Except, I hope it's not. I hope there is much more to see after this, even if I'm not here to see it." And with that, she was done.

"Godspeed, Kip," the voice said.

"Crown out."

As soon as the transmission was cut, she threw herself onto the control deck in front of her and cried her heart out. Every tear she had been holding in for the past few hours, for the past few months of traveling, and the past few years in training, came out in that moment. But it only took a few seconds for her to regain her composure. She may have needed that, any person would have, but not many people could get back on point as quickly as Apolena.

She put on her restraints and got ready for the countdown. She was seconds out now and her vessel was in position. 5… 4… 3… 2… and ignition! Her vessel began vibrating. It was in the same location, but not in the same time, traveling back through years and years. On her view screen, she saw her planet changing slightly through the decades. After a few minutes, her speed increased. Hundreds of years per minute, thousands, hundreds of thousands, millions. The pressure! It was the pressure, more than anything. The normal feeling of a vacuum in eardrums when changing elevation, she felt all over her body. On her lungs, on her stomach, her arms, her chest, even her brain. She squeezed her eyes shut, as tight as she could. She let out a long scream, she had to release the pressure in any way possible.

Then the pressure stopped. And in the same second, everything else did as well. A strong light was shining through her screen. She saw the brightness through her closed eyes like the sun shining on a summer day. She opened them to see a sky on fire. Orange, yellow, spurts of red, all random but flowing in harmony, all around her. She looked behind her at the back screen, black, nothingness. She spun her head back around to the front. This was the big bang. This blazing sea of incandescence, this was the start of it all. And what a beauty it was. She couldn't yet discern anything, not enough time had passed. It was just a fiery explosion. Her equipment took the necessary readings. Now it was time. Time to go back to when no one had gone before.

She set the time navigations on the vessel, and before hitting the button, she took a deep breath and closed her eyes.

"Blast off," she whispered.

I. Ashmawey

She didn't feel anything. Eyes still shut tight, muscles still stressed, she waited. But nothing happened.

"You may open your eyes, so that we can speak," a voice said.

She opened her eyes. She wasn't in her vessel anymore. But she was still on her same, oversized comfortable chair. She was in a white space, no walls, no ceiling, and no end. White in every direction, a white abyss. Standing in front of her was her commanding officer at NASA. The one who had been speaking to her via communication controls.

"What are... where am I?"

"I am not who you think I am," he said.

"You're my comman—" she started.

"No, I am not. I am in this familiar form so as not to scare you," he said to her. She nodded her head. "Please listen closely Apolena," he started. "You are the first of mankind to reach this stage. A stage that so much is dependent on. The completion of the cosmos."

"What do you mean, completion?" she asked. She felt her heart now racing at incomparable speeds. She panted quickly, taking very short breaths.

"Your time on earth was limited. It began with the big bang. And it ends now. The plan, all along, was to leave humanity to progress until the moment that you found your way to the beginning. That would be the time that things on earth would end, and you would move on to the next stage. All of you."

"Are ..." she hesitated. "Are you..."

"No, I am not the Creator. But it is, in fact, time for you to meet Him. For all of you to meet Him."

11

The Observer

I. Ashmawey

T he agreed upon time was 100 years. That was how long the AMEBOG, the latest scientific achievement in artificial intelligence, was commissioned to observe. The four chief engineers, dubbed the Patrons, spent two years finding the correct family and household to install the AMEBOG—the Artificial Mechanical Electro-functioning Body Of Growth—into. It had to be an American family that was typical, in every sense of the word. A family that represented and defined the average American home. Much to the Patrons' surprise, such a household deemed more difficult to find than anticipated. An average number of individuals was the easy part, average income was a piece of cake, but average behaviors... there was the rub. For what dictates average? Normal? Ordinary?

As it turned out, there were a lot of aspects of 'average' that the Patrons chose not to include. The average household had a staggering amount of domestic violence; they did not want AMEBOG to know that. The average household also had a dysfunctional marriage; they did not want AMEBOG to know that either. The average American household had children who resented their parents; they absolutely did not want AMEBOG to know that, as it would have been strictly against their mission statement.

As such, after a review of over 2,000 average families, the Patrons decided to tweak their goal. They would now be searching for the *ideal* average family; the annexed word, of course, being entirely subjective. This did not make the search any easier for them, mind you. But it did make the search more focused. And, for the Patrons, less depressing.

This was precisely the reason the Patrons opted to install the AMEBOG in a brick and mortar home rather than connect it to the internet and allow it to feed off of unfiltered, unvetted, and incorrect information. You see, the goal of the AMEBOG was simple, but we did not know it. That was the thing about the Patrons, they were most mysterious. What kind of person, particularly an engineer or inventor, would create something knowing they will not see it come to fruition in their lifetime? And if you did find one such person, would you ever find four? All four Patrons, two men, and two women, were highly regarded as four of the most gifted minds on the face of the planet. You can imagine the conspiracy theories about the AMEBOG's purpose. And the bets; a lot of bets placed in those decades. Whatever the intentions of the Patrons, which the whole world wanted to know, would remain secret until the AMEBOG completes its observation.

So it was this family that lived in Lebanon, Kansas that was chosen for this tremendous step in artificial intelligence discovery. Right in the geographic center of the contiguous United States lived a family of three: man, wife, and four-year-old son. This son, entirely unbeknownst to him, was volunteered into a position that he would have to comply with for his entire life. And he too would never see the fruits of it. Granted, there was some money involved. It was not enough to make a living, as technically there was no work to be done by the family. All they had to do was live in the same house for their entire lives, and carry on living as usual. Their son would have to continue living in that same home and insist at least one of his children live in the same home as well. One hundred consecutive years of observation were needed to gather enough data for the AMEBOG's mission. There would be absolutely no exceptions to that directive and the Patrons paid dearly to make sure that would be implemented.

The woman's name was Katelyn Hale, her husband was Brenden Hale. Their son was Austin, an energetic four-year-old who could throw a ball for hours and hours. Brendan was an accountant, and Katelyn a kindergarten teacher. Their home was average, their salaries were average, their life was ideal and average; they fit perfectly.

And so the AMEBOG was installed in their small, three bedroom ranch in Lebanon, Kansas, on December 31st at the stroke of midnight. The heart of this device was a CPU unit buried thirty-five feet under the ground and protected by two feet of thick stainless steel, further covered by a cement enclosure. This was coupled with cameras in the family room, living room, kitchen, and hallways. The adults of the family signed an exuberant amount of paperwork in return for being part of this tremendous undertaking.

And so it was.

And the one hundred years began.

For the first few months, the family had a tremendously difficult time getting used to it. No matter what they were doing, no matter how engulfed they were in their day to day activities, they would always be aware that somebody was watching them. But there was nobody watching, only the AMEBOG. An artificial being whose memory banks no human had access to, or ever would have access to. The data compiled was to remain absolutely confidential forever.

But still, whenever any member of the family would come close to losing their tempers due to the pressures of everyday life, they would look up and see the red light on the cameras, and suddenly things would calm down. Eventually, Brenden covered the red light, he couldn't take it anymore. And within a year, the family was acting normal again, completely forgetting the AMEBOG existed.

The years passed, and Austin grew. Much of the hype around the AMEBOG died out. A few articles would appear here and there but people mostly forgot about its existence, especially after the last of the Patrons passed away. Their final words were, "The AMEBOG will answer everything."

Austin did not have any problems with what his parents signed him up for. On the contrary, he was happy with the extra income coming in. Brendan and Katelyn passed away, and Austin had children of his own; twin girls, Miley and Christina. And on their seventy-fourth birthday, they celebrated the completion of the AMEBOG's observation. Their father had passed away roughly a decade before that day. Not remembering its inception, he wasn't very intrigued by it to begin with. The twins were much more interested as they knew they had a good probability of witnessing its completion.

And on the final day, Christina came to visit her sister Miley who was residing in the home. Tens of people were there, all friends and family, waiting to see what would happen. A few reporters came by, but nothing major. All those who were alive when the Patrons began the project had passed away. Yesterday's excitement became today's history.

And so they counted down. And at the stroke of midnight, the observation was complete. A full minute passed and nothing had happened. Two minutes. Five. Ten. It was not until half an hour later that something happened. Someone walked in, a man in his mid-thirties. He was dressed in white pants and a white button down shirt. His short blond hair was combed to one side.

"Excuse us, who are you?" Miley asked, being the owner of the home.

"I am AMEBOG," the man said. This was met by tremendous laughter from everyone in the house. And then a sudden stopping of laughter when the man walked through the wall in the family room, and then back through it again. People's jaws dropped, all looking to each other confused. Some took a few steps back.

"Okay," Miley said apprehensively, "You're AMEBOG."

"I thank you for your time and your commitment to my creation," AMEBOG said, standing in front of the entire crowd of people present. "Without your help, I would not be here."

"Why were you created?" Christina asked. "We've been waiting, the whole world has been waiting, to find out."

"I will report my findings and my purpose tomorrow. It will be broadcast on all radio frequencies, across all news channels, and across all internet platforms."

"Wait! Wait a minute!" Miley said. "You're not supposed to report anything confidential about my family!"

"Absolutely. Nothing of the sort will be revealed, ma'am. I have nothing but the utmost respect for your family." And with that, AMEBOG disappeared. After waiting one hundred years, the world had to wait another day. And so they did. And the next day, the following was broadcast:

I am AMEBOG. For one hundred years I have observed an American household. I have concluded determining the purpose of life, and that is nothing more than moving things. One wakes up and moves the covers. They move their bodies from one place to another. They consume food, moving it from the table to their mouths, and back out into the earth. They move money and material things. Every action a human being does is nothing more than moving things, with the motivation or belief that this will advance their existence.

Those are my findings. As the Patrons have programmed me, I must say the following:

If you agree with my findings, then know that there is hope for artificial intelligence to one day replace humanity. As humanity does nothing that artificial intelligence cannot. As such, work on it. Advance it. Invest time, money, and effort into it. If you do not agree with my findings, then know that even after one hundred years of programming by observation, artificial intelligence will never be human. So stop trying to make it so, and rather advance your own, inter-human relationships.

Thank you.

12

The Enigmatic Conversation

I. Ashmawey

She had only a few minutes before needing to join her parents for supper. And so, for those fleeting moments, Irraisa Amaya would satisfy her latest obsession: chatting online. In the few months that online chatting services had become known, Irraisa—an extremely intelligent and bright twelve-year-old girl living in Rochester Hills, Michigan—had dominated all the available platforms.

In the real world, she was socially awkward. If anyone at school spoke to Irraisa, her face would flush to a strawberry red and blood would rush to her head so fast, she would have difficulty hearing the person speaking to her. While giving a biographical presentation to her class dressed as Annie Oakley, her nose started bleeding profusely down her chin. The students weren't sure if it was part of the presentation or not, even the teacher couldn't tell. Her awkwardness did not at all hinder her academic performance however. She was gifted, and everyone knew it.

The online world gave Irraisa all the confidence she lacked in reality. For in the digital world, she could be anybody. Sometimes she wondered why she so desperately wanted to be someone else. She was a very kind person and smart like we said. She was average height for her age, wavy black hair, usually in a ponytail. A Native hue, as her family descended from the Navajo tribe.

Regardless, for Irraisa, being online was freeing. She chatted with anybody, and all who came in contact with her absolutely loved her. She had a great sense of humor and her intelligence made for great conversation. And after a rough school day of being bullied for being too smart, she could use the solace. You see, Irraisa wasn't just traditionally smart. And she wasn't just untraditionally smart like people who could calculate large math problems in their heads. Or untraditionally smart in that she had a photographic memory. Those things were actually old news to the majority of untraditionally smart people. On the grander scheme of things, they were forgettable.

No, what Irraisa had was different. Unbeknownst to her, the way her brain processed information was incredibly unique. And that was undoubtedly her greatest strength. When the teacher would ask the area of a circle, the smart students would answer with 3.14 multiplied by r^2. Irraisa however, well she would ask why it was so. Was it not arbitrary? Was it not simply because we defined it as such? It was, but *why* did we define it as such? While most would say Irraisa asked a lot of questions, a handful saw something special in her.

And so it was one evening in the few minutes before dinner that a chat popped up on her computer: *"Hello?"*

She wrote back: *"Hi. Irraisa, female, 12, Michigan. ASL?"*

He asked: *"ASL?"*

She responded: *"Yeah. Your age, gender, location. Ya know, ASL."*

He wrote: *"Oh. My name is Alex. I'm twelve years old. I live in Lawton, Oklahoma but I don't know where I am. I need help."*

"Of course you need help. Don't we all?" she whispered out loud. "But I don't buy that you're twelve."

Alex wrote: *"I'm stuck somewhere. I don't know how I got here."*

Irraisa wrote: *"I'm twelve. But I'm not stupid."*

Alex begged: *"Please call the police. Right now."*

Irraisa asked: *"Wait, are you serious?"*

Alex wrote: *"Yes. Please help me."*

Irraisa asked: *"Where are you exactly?"*

This didn't sound normal to Irraisa, none of it did. Somebody from school was pranking her, obviously. They had found out her screen name and were now going to torment her for some laughs. She couldn't have that. Not now, not here. This was her place, her sanctuary.

But still, what if? What if it wasn't fake?

"Irraisa!" her mom yelled from the kitchen. "Supper's ready, honey!"

"I'm coming, mom!" Irraisa yelled back.

Alex wrote: *"I don't know where I am. But it's a classroom. The door is locked and there are no windows. And there's a problem written on the blackboard."*

"Okay, someone's messing with me," Irraisa said to herself. A classroom. A problem written. And she was the smartest child in a hundred mile radius. Someone was either messing with her or needed help with their homework. It was decided, she was not going to entertain this any further.

Except...

She could not ignore a problem that needed solving.

Another side effect of being an absolute genius, she couldn't be introduced to a problem and not solve it. If she didn't dig her teeth into it, it could ruin her. Not that she was obsessive compulsive, it wasn't about completion. But it would bother her beyond belief to know that there was a problem in existence that her mind has not had the pleasure of defeating. She at least needed to know what the problem was. If she knew she could solve it easily, she probably wouldn't care and would ignore it. If she couldn't solve it, she would figure out how to solve it. Period.

She wrote: *"What's the problem?"*

Alex wrote: *"I don't understand it. I'll read it: Mr. Smith has two children. At least one of them is a boy. What is the probability that both children are boys?"*

Irraisa wrote: *"That's all it says?"*

Alex said: *"Beneath it says: 'Solve to be freed.' Isn't it just fifty percent? I think it's fifty percent, I'm just too scared to do anything right now. I don't know why this is happening. Or how I even ended up here."*

Irraisa wrote: *"No. It's not."*

Alex wrote: *"Of course it is! The chances of having a boy or girl are always fifty-fifty!"*

Irraisa wrote: *"That's not the question. The problem didn't say he was going to have a second child and asked what the probability was. The problem said that he already had two, and then asked for the probability."*

Alex wrote: *"But how is that different?"*

Irraisa wrote: *"Combinations of Male and Female are four: MM, FF, MF, and FM."*

Alex wrote: *"Okay, so twenty-five percent then."*

Irraisa wrote: *"No, we know it's not FF, cancel that out. You're left with three choices. And MM is one of those three. The answer is one-third."*

There was a silence. No one wrote anything.

What was she doing? She knew exactly what was going on. Someone who clearly was not twelve was trying to solve a much more advanced statistics problem and was mooching off of her. Probably the older sibling of one of her classmates. And this person was a liar, yet she was still helping them. The worst part was she had absolutely no reason to; but she still did.

Was she just that good of a person? Or was she naive?

Alex finally wrote: *"Okay. I'm going to write your answer."*

Another few seconds passed by with no response. Silence. Silence. Then…

Alex wrote: *"The door opened!!"*

Irraisa wrote: *"Great. I'm happy for you. Now, who are you?"*

But to that, she got no response.

"Of course. God, I'm stupid. At least have the courtesy to say thank you."

Across the country, in Lawton, Oklahoma, a twelve-year-old boy woke up from a coma.

"Mom?"

"Oh honey!" The mother embraced her son. "Thank God. Oh, thank God."

I. Ashmawey

"Mom... someone was helping me. I was solving a problem," Alex said.
"What? Oh honey, you were dreaming," the mother said.
"No..." Alex said, with a heavy head. "No... her name was Irraisa."

And back in Rochester Hills, Michigan, Irraisa Amaya had not even begun to learn the power of her own mind.

13

The Unconditional Soldier

I. Ashmawey

"None of this should be happening."

That was the only thing I could think in that moment. I didn't know how or why. I couldn't describe the feeling any further as it was the first time I had experienced it. I knew little, but what I did know was simple: none of it should have happened.

I couldn't tell you if she was beautiful or not. I couldn't—I wasn't capable of knowing even for myself. But here is what I did know: she did something strange to my entire being. I had a genuine need for her. For her existence. For her touch. You see, that's what it all started with: a touch. My hand touched hers entirely by accident. It was more of a brush to be more accurate. But it instigated an explosion inside my body.

That didn't change the reality however that none of this, absolutely none of this, should have happened.

My number was 194563. That number was not random, but rather my birth number. I was the 194,563rd person to be born into the Corinth Program. In the program, I was born, bred, raised, and served. I served honorably and fully dedicated. All that was fine, all that was good. Corinth took the best care of us and it was a phenomenal life. There was no hiding what we were, the program was very honest with us. We were engineered soldiers. No parents, so no one to grieve our loss. No family, so no citizens resisting a war. And most importantly, no emotions, so things never got messy. We were engineered without them. We didn't even know the word 'emotion' until I discovered it by accident. For decades, there were no problems as far as anyone was concerned.

The problem was her.

Her number was 194523, and she was in my faction. I had known her and many others for my entire life. And all those before me in the Corinth Program had known each other as well. I had met 194523 before, many times. All soldiers ate with their faction, trained with their faction, and rested with their faction. Entertainment was not something we required.

And to prove it to us, the program had offered us entertainment on many occasions and we refused it. If our bodies were not being constantly physically challenged, we did not feel accomplishment. What most Outsiders (our term for people not in the program) did not know was that the human body is limitless. Let me be clear on something, besides being born without a mother or father, our physical bodies were not genetically engineered to be any different than those of an Outsider. The alteration happened in our minds, not our bodies.

Yet, our bodies had reached strengths superhero comicbook authors could not have imagined. We lifted vehicles above our heads, sometimes balancing them with one arm. We all, without exception, ran the mile in under two minutes. Some of us attained such high speeds when running that our feet spent more time in the air than touching the ground. This was all without special supplements and without any medical or mechanical enhancements. Simply the fruit of the labors of concentrating one's time, mind, and focus on improving their physical body.

We had a library with handpicked books for our perusal. Not many of us read. I personally never spent any free time reading, until I met her. But we both wanted to know what it was we were experiencing. Certainly, our superior officers wouldn't tell us. And none of the entertainment—movies, songs, comics—we were given provided any answers. So we had to look elsewhere.

We began spending most of our time in the library going through endless novels trying to find anything that sounded like what we were experiencing. The library seating was not very comfortable, perhaps because no one complained. It was a small, damp room with four walls and large built-in bookshelves reaching from the floor to the ceiling. In the center of the room was a large bean bag for seating. And like everything else at the Corinth Program, it was a room entirely of a gray color. Gray walls, carpet, and bookshelves. Granted it made spending hours in the room devoid of any comfort, but we were determined to find an answer to our puzzlement.

It was after more than a year of reading all the physiological and biological books available that I finally came across something written by a man named Charles Dickens. It was the first and only fiction book I found. And in a story about a boy named David Copperfield who grew up without his father, Dickens wrote: "She was more than human to me. She was a Fairy, a Sylph, I don't know what she was—anything that no one ever saw, and everything that everybody ever wanted. I was swallowed up in an abyss of love in an instant. There was no pausing on the brink; no looking down, or looking back; I was gone, headlong, before I had sense to say a word to her."

Love?

Whatever that was, it was happening to me. The moment I had finished reading the passage, I immediately went back to the beginning and reread it. And again. And a fourth time. Charles Dickens knew me, and he knew exactly what I was going through. It was like he had opened my mind and body, read me, and dictated it word for word to the rest of the world.

After finishing the passage for a fifth time, something happened to me. There was water. A salty, stinging water fell from my eyes that burned my cheeks. I didn't understand what was happening, but I wanted more of it, and so more came out. So much more, that it scared me. I felt like for years I had carried so much of it inside me and finally the faucet had been opened. But with every passing second, the heaviness in my chest got lighter. 194523 was worried about me until I handed her the book and she read the same passage. The exact same phenomena then happened to her. We were scared but did not want to rush into anything. We waited till we had regained our strength after a long, peaceful sleep. One that we had never experienced anything like before.

The next day, we went to see the commanding chief of our faction in his office. His name was Father 106.

"Father, thank you for seeing us," I said.

"Anything for my children. My door is always open. Sit please, both of you," he gestured. He wore the same uniform as us, gray pants, gray button down shirt, and a gray cap. We were all the same, always. "How can I help the both of you?" 194523, or 23 as I have jokingly called her since we have experienced these strange phenomena, looked to me. I nodded to her to speak first.

"We believe we have experienced the phenomena of love," 23 said. Father 106's eyes shot open, pushing his eyebrows up, almost into his cap. They quickly went back to normal, too quickly actually. Then he smiled a most comforting smile. It seemed as though he was excited.

"Love?" he asked.

"Yes," I responded. "Too much for us to know how to handle."
He continued smiling. He crept up to the edge of his seat before asking, "What is love? I must hear it. From you."

"I can't describe it," 23 said.

"Neither can I, Father," I said.

"I see. Can you describe the events that transpired?" he asked.

"Well," I said, "when I first saw 23..."

"23?" Father 106 interrupted.

"194523. When I saw her, I knew that she was anything that no one ever saw, and everything that everybody ever wanted. And that is how I know that I have love for her," I explained.

Father 106's smile grew. He was certainly excited. "Where did you get that from?" he asked.

"Charles Dickens," I said.

"Of course," Father 106 said to himself. "The classics. I should have known.

Listen, you two. What you are both experiencing is a tremendous evolution. We didn't think it would happen within the Corinth Program. Some believed it may, but certainly not this soon."

"Father?" 23 questioned. "An evolution?

"What do you suggest we do, Father?" I asked.

"Well..." he sat back in his seat, looking up to the ceiling to think. "What would you do if I said you two must separate?" he asked.

"Impossible," I said without thinking. And I did not need to think. This would never happen.

"Never," 23 said. She took my hand, and I held hers tightly. Father 106 eyed us carefully and his smile only grew larger. What were we doing?! How was this already so strong that it completely took control of us? Love? Could love do all this? But it was as if we were under a spell. We had strings connected to us and puppeteers dictating our every move. Perhaps we were dictating each other's moves. I will never know.

"Good. Very good, my children. I dare say, I'm extremely happy for you both.

Then within a fraction of a second, Father 106, with a flare of his nostrils and fire in his eyes, pulled out a weapon and shot me in my heart. Where I knew that 23 lived. Before understanding what had happened, he did the same to 23. I fell to the ground on my back. 23 fell on top of me. I moved my hand to her face, and both our eyes closed.

Father 106 picked up a phone and dialed a number.

"Eliminate the entire flock. Contamination. Time to start from scratch. And this time, get rid of the classics. Those books make people feel things apparently."

14

One of Wisdom

"Mom?" the young boy said. "Should I judge people based on their actions or their beliefs? They both seem really close."

The mother put down her work, for she knew this was not a simple question to answer. Her son, barely ten, still opening his eyes to the world around him, was asking one of the most difficult questions she had ever heard posed. Not that she did not have answer, she did. And it was easy to comprehend. But she knew so many people lived their entire lives not asking this question specifically because they did not want to follow the answer.

More importantly however, even when a parent knows the answer, the difficulty is in deciding how to pose it to the child.

"Sit with me, honey," the mother said as she sat on the comfortable love seat in their cozy family room. "There was once a man named Water."

Her son laughed. "Of course not! You must be joking with me." His mother did not respond with anything but a solemn face. He wondered to himself if this was his mother's response to his question. Was she implying that he should not judge based on someone's name?

"His name was Water," she continued. "He thought he was wise, he always did. Till he learned of a man wiser than he named Green."

"Oh come on, now. Water and Green? Mom, where are you getting these names?" he asked with a chuckle.

"Water went to Green and told him he believed he had much to learn from him, as he knew that Green had knowledge from God Himself. And so Water asked to watch him, follow him, and learn from him. Green didn't like the idea, for he knew Water would not be able to withstand the challenges ahead of them. Water vehemently insisted, and Green eventually agreed but under one condition: Water would never question any of Green's actions. Water agreed to this condition, as he felt lucky to even be going along.

The two began their trek by taking a trail into the heavy forest. After a number of uneventful hours passing, Water began to lose interest. Green did nothing out of the ordinary; he hunted some game, he picked some fruit, he even took a short nap under a tree. All the while, Water was following his every move. Eventually, they came across a young boy. The boy was carrying a sack which he put down under a tree before running after a rabbit, chasing it here and there. Just as Water was about to approach the boy to help him catch the rabbit, he noticed Green, out of the corner of his eye, approach the boy's sack, open it, take out some gold coins, and put them into his pockets."

"What!? Why would he steal from the boy?" the son asked.

"That's exactly what Water wondered. He yelled out to Green, asking him why he'd steal from a young boy. You can even say he attacked him. Of course, Green didn't take that well. He reminded Water of his vow. Begrudgingly, Water apologized, and they moved on. A while later, they exited the forest and made their way to a seaport. Green stood at the edge of the bay and they both watched a beautiful ship make port. Its owners disembarked and made their way into the city. They seemed like perfectly amicable people. As soon as they were out of sight, Green took an axe and went at the ship. Trashing it and destroying it from every side."

"That seems cruel," the boy commented.

"Too right, it did," his mother responded. "Water did not disagree with you. He told him that the owners of the ship seemed like nothing but kind and righteous people. How can ruining their property be an act of wisdom?! Of course, you can imagine Green's reaction."

"I'm sure he reminded him of his vow," the boy said.

"Precisely. To which Water did not disagree. As such, he promised that if he slipped even one more time, he would leave Green and not follow him anymore. So they went on. Next, they traveled to a small town a few miles away. They entered the town and asked for hospitality, just a place to rest and a bite to eat. The people of the town did not like strangers, so vehemently refused, and rudely kicked them out. Water and Green didn't want to argue, so they made their way out of the town. But as they crossed the way, they found a brick fence surrounding the city that was decrepit and broken down. Water walked right past it. Green, on the other hand, stopped and worked to rebuild the fence. Water, of course, was furious. He asked him why he cared to rebuild a fence to help people who treated them so poorly."

"Water keeps forgetting," the boy said.

"And so Green had had enough. He told Water he knew he wouldn't be patient enough to journey with him. And so now, he would tell Water the reasons behind his actions. The boy he stole from in the forest, Green had knowledge of his past. The boy was a thief, and everything he had did not belong to him.

As for the ship, it belonged to good people. But they were set to travel to a land whose King takes any ship he likes by force. So Green had decided to scar the ship so that the King wouldn't like it, and it would thus be saved for the owners.

And lastly, the fence. Beneath the fence was a buried treasure that belonged to two young boys in the city. They were good boys, and so were their parents. In their olden age, they will discover the buried treasure and put it to good use."

"Hm," the boy said. "So what you're trying to say is, you shouldn't judge people's actions. Because you never know the true motive behind them."

"That is a true statement," the mother replied.

"Okay, so I should judge people based on their beliefs then. Because if the belief is wrong, it's wrong. It can't be misunderstood."

"Well, that's one way to look at it. And I'm not going to say that people may change their beliefs in the future. However, what if you change yours?"

"What do you mean?" the boy asked.

"Well, no one is born knowing everything. So, as you grow older, you learn different things and are exposed to more of the world. As such, your beliefs of what is right and wrong could change. Or else, you wouldn't be growing."

"Okay," the boy said, not knowing where she was going with this.

"So perhaps your own beliefs will change. And you will see that people you thought were wrong, actually weren't wrong at all," she explained.

The boy scrunched his face. You could tell he was squeezing his brain rather hard. His mother watched him turn his head slightly, one way and then the other, as if he was talking to himself; remembering his initial question to his mother.

"So, I shouldn't judge people based on their actions, as I'll never know all their motives. Clearly, I shouldn't judge people based on their beliefs, as my own beliefs might change," the boy said.

"You're right," the mom said with a smile.

"So... when should I judge people?" he asked.

"I'll let you answer that question," the mother said. She tucked him into bed, kissed him goodnight, and turned off the lights. And in the dark, the boy thought to himself. And in the dark, on that important night, he learned a lesson. And in the dark, he decided how he would interact with people for the rest of his life.

I. Ashmawey

15

Technicolor

It was September 1, 1916. My legs dangled above the floor as I sat on a red stool at the counter of the ice cream shop. "The Sunshine of Your Smile" by John Mc-Cormack played on the radio. I had exactly five pennies in my palm, count them. I was pretty good at counting money considering I was only six years old. I piled all five pennies on top of each other on the counter and slid them across to Mr. Montague.

"What'll it be, Billy?" he asked with his cheerful smile. Mr. Montague was an old, old man. Probably older than my grandpa at the time. And skinnier than a straw.

"Ice cream float please," I asked politely.

"Oh, I'm sorry, Billy. Ice cream floats are ten cents. For five, I can get you a good scoop of ice cream though!" he said with an uplift in his voice.

"Okay! Vanilla please." Mr. Montague nodded his head and went off. I looked across the counter at my reflection in the huge, wall to wall mirror. My curly hair had a mind of it's own. If my mom had been there, she would have licked her palm and patted down as many of my stray hairs as she could.

"Here you go, Billy my boy." Mr. Montague came back with an ice cream float anyway! I couldn't believe my eyes that were probably popping out of their sockets. What a swell guy he was. I wrapped my lips around the straw and went at it. Whenever I saw a straw, I thought of Mr. Montague. And whenever I saw Mr. Montague, I thought of straws. "Easy does it, sonny boy. You don't wanna go too fast, your brain will hurt."

I didn't listen. "It's just too good, sir!" I looked down into my drink as I slurped it up. I loved watching the dark soda get lower as the scoop of white ice cream got smaller.

The song on the radio stopped abruptly. "This just in. Stay tuned tonight at seven for an outstanding announcement by the new, international corporation, Technicolor. The announcement is sure to change the world as we know it."

"Did you hear that, Billy boy?!" Mr. Montague asked. "I've read all about it in the papers. It's a complete secret, they're not telling anyone what the announcement is. But I'll tell you Billy, whatever it is, it will change our world. That's right, change our world!"

I didn't respond. I didn't say much in general, I was young and an observer. At the moment, I cared more about my ice cream float that I had gotten at half price. It was delicious! I slurped up the remaining soda that was now fully infused with the vanilla flavor. Before I had finished, Mr. Montague had placed a long spoon next to my glass. I picked up all the remaining ice cream in one spoonful and gulped it down. It froze my teeth cold, but it was worth it.

"Thank you, Mr. Montague!" I said as I hopped down from the stool. It was a good foot high fall before I felt the floor. "I'm off to the pictures now. I'm meeting Ralph and we're going to see 20,000 Leagues Under The Sea. It should be swell." I waved goodbye as I stepped out the door.

It was a hot day in sunny Southern California. And there was a strange energy outside; I felt it as soon as my eyes got accustomed to the bright, blazing sun. Everybody was out on the streets, talking, chattering, discussing something very seriously. Some were so excited, they were yelling. Like something big was happening. Every mouth was in an ear. They were probably talking about the Technicolor announcement, the one no one knew anything about yet. I never understood why adults talked so much, they always seemed to have something to say about everything. And if they really couldn't think of anything, they'd at least talk about how they didn't have anything to say. It was very confusing.

Nevertheless, what did I care? I had a movie to watch! My father had read me the story by Jules Verne twice. I didn't understand it all, but I loved what bits I did. And I couldn't wait to see Captain Nemo in action with his tremendous submarine. A ship unlike anything the world had ever seen before!

And so, as I sat in the cinema with Ralph, I worked hard to minimize my blinking! I couldn't miss a single frame of this earth-shattering amazingness. Seeing the Nautilus, the electrically powered submarine, traveling across all the oceans exploring the worlds of the deep was alone enough to make it the best film ever made. But the scene where the Nautilus was attacked by an enormous, monstrous squid, that was something I would never forget for the rest of my life! The film was perfect in every way and completely worth finishing my weekly salary from delivering newspapers on.

"Wasn't that something?" I asked Ralph as we stepped out of the cinema room.

"You bet it was. That's exactly what I'm going to do when I grow up. I'm going to build me a Nautilus and explore the world! You can be my first mate, Billy."

"That sounds swell, Ralph," I responded.

"You bet. We'll start off exploring the Arctic. My old man told me they got polar bears there that can swallow a person up whole. Ferocious things," Ralph continued. And he kept going. Ralph had the amazing ability to talk nonstop. He could also jump from topic to topic without taking a break. I didn't continue listening though. Instead, I watched the adults talking about the film. I wondered what they thought of it. I slowly made my way closer to a group of adults standing next to the concession stand so I can listen better. Ralph didn't even notice, he just followed me over, still talking about his future plans. I got close enough to hear them without making myself obvious.

"I'm telling you," one of the adults said, "once Technicolor releases their new invention, watching a picture like what we just saw now would be an entirely different experience! Can you imagine? Seeing the mysterious underwater worlds in an entirely different way!" The adult was talking with his arms flying above his head. And they all shared his excitement, every single one.

"If it's true, it's going to be something else! I hope you're right about the invention."

"I can't wait. It'll change our world!" And so on.

I still didn't understand. I hadn't a clue what this invention would be or why it would change anything at all. But apparently, some people knew what it would be. And everyone seemed to agree it was going to change our world.

Later that night, my parents talked about the very same thing. They each had their own guesses on what the announcement was going to be. But at some point, just as my Dad was chewing his green beans, they both decided it was best to stop guessing and just wait and see.

It was only half an hour afterward, as we each enjoyed a slice of hot apple pie with a scoop of ice cream (unknown to my parents, it was my second ice cream scoop that day) that we sat around the radio and listened intently. After what seemed like forever, the announcer finally came on and introduced the guest for the evening.

"Ladies and gentlemen, I am Daniel Frost Comstock, the President of Technicolor. We'd like to take this moment to thank you for joining us on this historic evening. I will not delay a moment, as this day is sure to be momentous. Ladies and gentlemen, we at Technicolor have invented something new. That invention is color." My mother gasped at hearing this. She looked to my father whose eyes had a wonderful gleam. Mr. Comstock continued. "Since the dawn of mankind, our world has been composed of two colors, black, and white, and different shades in between. In exactly one minute, we will flip the switch on our new machine. At that moment, the entire world will be converted to color. Everything, ladies and gentlemen, boys and girls, will change in a fraction of a second.

"You will be able to look at the people around and enjoy their different colors and different shades. You will be able to look at your belongings and see all the hues. And most importantly, you will be able to look at nature, look at our world, and see chromaticity that we have yet to see as a species. And with that, we have thirty seconds left. Begin the countdown..."

I left my parents and ran outside. It was night. I looked up to the sky. I wanted to see. I needed to see. I knew it was dark, and I knew that it would still be dark after, but still, the first thing I wanted to see was...

And then it happened, the sky. It lit up. How did it go from dark, to still dark but with color? It was all shades of purple, blue, and black. Stars shined like glistening diamonds on a dark velvet canvas. My world would never be the same, and the possibilities of my future were endless.

16

Darwin's Grandchildren

"The question that we hope to answer here, ladies and gentlemen, is simple: can evolution occur again? We here, at Darwin Cybertronics—the largest leading medical artificial intelligence manufacturer on the planet—dedicate every day to making the answer to that question an overwhelming yes." The crowd wildly cheered. All thirty thousand employees of Darwin Cybertronics, government officials, investors, interested citizens, watched and cheered as Maverick Stonegate, CEO and founder of the company, spoke of his corporation's newest invention. "Tomorrow morning will be the dawn of a new era. The next stage of evolution for our species, for our planet. Join us tomorrow to witness history."

And with that, Maverick Stonegate ended his iconic speech. One that people would remember for many years.

It was in his ninety thousand square foot mansion outside the city that Rose Montanosa sat quietly in his study, waiting for him to arrive. A young reporter with long black hair tied neatly in a professional bun and a pressed black suit, this was Rose's most important interview to date. She was still young in her career and building a portfolio of interviews. The study doors opened and Maverick Stonegate, the young and vibrant CEO with perfect combed back brown hair and hazel eyes, walked in and hung his coat up on the coat stand before shaking Rose's hand.

"I'm terribly sorry for being tardy, Miss...?"

"Rose Montanosa."

"Montanosa. Yes. Well, I do apologize," he said with a charming smile as he took the seat near Rose. He clearly made it a point to sit on the same side of the desk as her. She recognized that immediately, and understood his motive in doing so: personality. It changes the tone of an interview entirely. "The speech went a bit longer than anticipated."

"Yes I was listening to it here on my phone, Mr. Stonegate," she said.

"Maverick. Even Mav, if you prefer," he offered.

"Maverick," she complied. "How about we start with the speech you gave?"

"Oh. Jumping right in, huh? Would you like something to drink?" he asked. Rose shook her head politely. "Very well." Rose could tell that he had initially intended on having a drink but changed his mind to match her. Instead, he re-situated himself in his chair. "Okay, the speech. Did you have a question concerning it?"

"I did. I mean, I do, in fact. You mentioned that this, what your corporation is conducting tomorrow morning, is the next stage in evolution."

"Absolutely," he stated.

"Well, I'll ask plainly. How do you figure?" she asked. She followed up her question immediately with a smile to show intent. She wasn't trying to be rude. She was simply doing her job of being inquisitive.

"Well," he began, "how would you define evolution, Miss Montanosa?"

"I'm not a biologist, as you know," Rose started. She cleared her throat. "But you have natural selection and adaptation. Natural selection being when a certain trait is better for survival, so members with that trait prevail. Adaptation being when instead, members slowly start forming that trait. Adapting."

"I think you're absolutely correct," Maverick smiled. "As you know, I'm not a biologist either. But let's talk about adaptation. Before snakes slithered, they had limbs similar to those of lizards. To better adapt to their environment of small holes in the ground, they lost their legs. Or the textbook example of the long-necked giraffe. The evolution of the giraffe's neck occurred so the animal could reach leaves in taller trees. All basic stuff, right?" Rose nodded. "Right. So all we're doing here at Darwin Cybertronics is adaptation. The human body is feeble and frail. It's how we are, we're not built to last. All we're doing here is allowing us now… to last."

"By making hybrid human androids," Rose said, sternly.

"A human cannot be a hybrid anything, Miss Montanosa. It is not possible. We're human, it's what we are. But we do employ much of what an android is, I suppose."

"Okay. So how is that adaptation? Adaptation is natural, and it happens over generations," Rose asked.

"Is this not natural?" Maverick asked. "What is natural? It's us, Rose. We, as a species, have evolved. And we, as a species, have created ways for us to adapt. This is no different than the giraffe spreading its neck further and further, and the ones that spread the furthest, survived. We're part of nature, Rose. So anything we do is considered natural."

"What if this isn't what the next stage of evolution should be?" Rose asked.

"Who's to say, Rose?" Maverick responded. "I mean, what are you expecting to happen? Are you thinking that in a million years, humans would have eight fingers or three eyes and it would just happen gradually the way it did before? Who's to say?"

"Maybe what you're doing is disrupting the natural evolution of our race. Did you think of that?" she asked.

"If it wasn't supposed to happen, it wouldn't happen," he responded. That made Rose snicker. "Oh, you think it's funny? You're one of those people that be-lieve that humanity needs to start from scratch, huh? Begin evolution all over again?"

"No. I just believe that perhaps we're looking for evolution in the wrong places."

Maverick nodded his head slowly, while fixating his eyes on her. "You're not a reporter, are you, Miss Montanosa?"

"No. And my name isn't Montanosa. Or Rose. I just needed to speak to the man that I believe is contributing to the downfall of my species." She stood up, and without saying another word, left his mansion and went home. Maverick Stonegate sat on the chair, thinking to himself, alone. But that didn't last long. A few seconds, and he got up and went about his evening.

The next morning, on a beautiful sunny beach, hundreds of reporters and thousands of spectators gathered on the sand in anticipation for the iconic reveal. A white, ten foot cubed building stood on the sand. In front of it, a small platform just large enough for Maverick to stand on. And there he stood, receiving the applause of a lifetime. Minutes passed, and people still applauded. As if he, himself, was doing them a favor. Perhaps he was. Perhaps he was changing their lives for the better. Prolonging them, increasing their quality, regrowing limbs, strengthening organs, adding things to their bodies they never could have dreamt of.

"Welcome all, to this fantastic occasion! I will not go through the introduc-tions, nor will I give any inspiring words. For the inspiration is what we will see now. Ladies and gentlemen, the next stage of human evolution!"

And with that short introduction, the white box behind Maverick broke down, each side falling to the sand. What was revealed was the world's first hu-mandroid. In the flesh, standing like any other human. From the outside, indis-tinguishable. Unless of course, you looked closely. For his skin cells were infused with microfiber metals, holding each molecule to the next. No aging, no tearing, no sagging. Inside, the heart was fully encased in a mechanical apparatus, doing all the work of the heart; adding decades, possibly centuries, to its pumping life. Liver, kidneys, stomach, intestines, all swapped with Cybertronics replacements. Each with a minimum life span guarantee. The bones were infused with liquid steel, never al-lowing breakage. The hair made of spider silk, strong and perfectly wavy. The mind connected to the internet, having access to every piece of information ever written. The eyes, cameras, constantly recording and analyzing images and processing them at phenomenal speeds.

The humandroid, the human at its best. The reactions were as expected: awe, praise, shock, happiness. Humans were one step closer to living forever. And more importantly, doing whatever they wanted to their bodies with little repercus-sions.

And on that beach, beyond the sand, something lurked. Coming out of the

I. Ashmawey

water where no one was looking, completely unexpected, unpredicted, and unannounced, a creature crawled on all fours. It looked like a fish, but had some sort of limbs. Its ancestors were swimmers, its descendants would be thinkers. It crawled on the sand and no one noticed. Because they were all staring at something else.

17

My Dinner with Brando

I. Ashmawey

We met at a Mexican restaurant, Don Jose's. He waited in his car till I arrived. I noticed it out front, tinted windows up with the engine still running. I tapped my fingers on the driver seat window—he probably fell asleep. Seconds later the engine was off, and he had stepped out. Gray hair slicked back with a black turtleneck under his gray blazer and baby blue jeans. He had gained just a bit of weight, still fit for his age though. He grabbed me violently to give me a hug, like it would have been repulsively wrong not to.

"How you doing, chief?" he asked. He fumbled as he attempted to give me a noogie that turned into him patting me on the head.

"I'm good, sir. I'm good."

"Don't... ugh... come on, now," he said as he threw his hands up and landed them on his waist. He gave a long exhale before scratching his forehead. "We're not going through this again. Marlon... or I kick you in the teeth. No sir, no mister, no diddly squat."

I nodded with a smile. We walked to the entrance of the strongly themed restaurant. From the outside, you knew that you were entering an authentic Mexican restaurant with the cold, adobe walls. "Why were you waiting in the car?" I asked. I knew the answer, but it was something to start our conversation for the evening.

"People. Some of them are like vermin, chief. I avoid them as long as I can," he responded.

"Yeah I guess being an actor ruins people for you indefinitely," I said.

"No, it's not being an actor, it's being a celebrity. Celebrity worship ostracizes reality. And this horrific adulation is everywhere," he responded with vigor. Speaking through his clenched teeth. We stepped into the festive restaurant. I held up two fingers to the hostess who immediately recognized my friend. She failed miserably at hiding her smile. We were led to the furthermost back of the restaurant to a small booth. Now, I've always known that Marlon loved escapism in all its forms: books, movies, art. And there were a number restaurants that actually offered that as well. But few did it as well as Don Jose's.

From the moment you walked in, you felt like you were in old Mexico. It was designed as if it was a town plaza with adobe buildings all around the side, enclosing a "town square." And in the middle of the square, was a beautiful fountain with the tables surrounding it. Each wall was like a different building. One was the home of The Don himself. Another was the traditional Mexican oven where an old lady was making tortillas. A third was a wall donned (pun intended) with flags. They really did an amazing job taking you out of wherever you were and putting you where they wanted you to be.

"Chips, please. A lot of chips," Marlon asked the hostess. She giggled at him, and her head jumped up and down like a duck as she nodded. "You see chief, the craze around political messiahs, athletes, musicians, or the devotion of millions of people to inspirational speakers, is all part of the yearning to see ourselves in those we worship. In short, we want to be like them, and to make them like us. The sad part is we try to be like them in the worst of ways."

"What do you mean?" I asked. "How do people try to be like them?"

"Well, they don't try the right things, I'll tell you that much," he huffed. "They don't try to be good people. They don't try to be altruistic. If altruism, religion, kindness, or The Purpose Driven Life won't make us a celebrity, then reality television will. Everyone is waiting for their cue to walk on stage and be lavishly admired."

One of the chips carriers brought us a tray of fresh tortilla chips. Marlon held up a finger, asking her for another tray, to which she obliged. He immediately dug in.

"Best food in the world. I always like to imagine the corn field where my food was grown. I read once that one should always be mindful while doing anything, but especially while eating," Marlon explained. I love how he talked to me about things as if I absolutely did not know them. It was funny and adorable at the same time. "This article in particular described mindfulness while eating a raisin. That you should spend time first looking at the raisin, noticing its shape and feeling its texture between your fingertips. Then when you put it in your mouth, don't chew right away. Move it between your teeth then let it roll on your tongue." He demonstrated with a chip as he explained. "As you chew it slowly, savor the taste. Imagine the food growing in the field. Imagine the farmer picking the corn. I like doing that with these tortilla chips but it's a little bit harder when you're eating a heavily processed food.

"I guess you can imagine that you're eating a vegetable and being healthy. It's not too much of a stretch. But imagine if I was eating a Swiss roll or a Twinkie. I could swear there is zero real food in those things. But they're just so damn tasty." He continued taking in more chips than he can possibly swallow. Only pausing to occasionally dip them in salsa or to put more salt on top of the already very salty chips.

"Marlon, why is it that people are celebrity crazed though? I mean, what started it?" I asked.

"Chief, the camera has created a culture of celebrity while the internet has created a culture of socio-connection. As the two technologies congregate, the two cultures betray a common instinct," he said. I had difficulty understanding. I didn't know if I was dumb or maybe he was speaking in tongues. "Okay, celebrity and socio-connection are both ways of becoming famous, right? This is what the contemporary person wants. They want to be recognized and connected: they want to be visible. If not to the millions on Big Brother or American Idol, then to the thousands on Twitter, Facebook, or Instagram. This is the value that validates them, this is how they become genuine to themselves: to be seen by others. They are only as important as the number of people that see them. The great modern fear of today is anonymity. Lionel Trilling said... have you read Lionel Trilling?" he asked. I shook my head. "Freaking, read Lionel Trilling! No joke. He said that the property that grounded the self in Romanticism was sincerity, and in Modernism was authenticity. If he was alive today, he would say that in the dystopia of Post-Modernism, it is visibility."

"But fame in itself isn't the enemy, right?" I chimed in.

"It's not that. It is this false social reality that has skewed the average person's perception of fame. Hedonism and fortune are worshipped on shows such as the Kardashians and The Real Housewives of Whatever. The American oligarchy becomes the characters we watch on television and want to be like. This life is dangled in front of us like a beacon, like the carrot to the donkey. The working classes, composed of millions of struggling Americans, are not in this gated community. Because they can't find the key? No, it's because they're too lazy and too busy observing to ever get up and make a damn key. People are left then, when they cannot compete with this life, with feelings of worthlessness. The flamboyant characters on television, movies, talk shows, professional wrestling, evangelical pastors, and the assortment of self-help bestsellers authored by motivational speakers are hawked to them, promising to fill up the emptiness in their own lives. What's worse, celebrity culture encourages everyone to think of themselves as potential celebrities, as possessing unique and unacknowledged gifts. It creates then, a culture of narcissism."

A waitress came up to us, grinning from ear to ear.

"What can I get you two this evening?" she asked.

"I'll have the enchiladas. One chicken, one beef. My friend will have the beef burrito, wet. Right, chief?" he asked me. I nodded. "But hurry please, we're starving. Oh, and two diet cokes with no ice," he said as he stuffed a few more chips into his mouth.

"Do you think there's anything good on television today?" I asked.

"Well. This whole exposition on the internet, it's terrible, chief. Celebrity culture today is primarily presented on the internet, many of which encourage a dark voyeurism into other people's humiliation and pain. Honesty and sharing are qualities that will always be voted off a show. Which by the way, is a perversion of morality. These shows teach that life is a brutal world of unsullied competition. In America, this structure has reached the point where a man who can throw an orange ball through a hoop with more accuracy than anyone else gains access to the President of the United States. A man that can rap better than others can have dinner with FLOTUS.

"On top of that, degradation as entertainment is the fetid underside to the allure of celebrity culture. We are transfixed by the spectacle of humiliation and debasement that comprise lurid television shows, you know which ones. Every year, there's a new one. But they're all the same. It is glee of sadistic impunity, the same impulse that drove crowds to the Roman Colosseum, to the pillory and the stocks, to public hangings, and to traveling freak shows."

"Okay but, not to toot your own horn or anything, but not all celebrities are bad. Right? I mean, you've done good things with it, haven't you?" I threw in there. Our food arrived just that second, excellent timing at Don Jose. Piping hot plates, and cheese perfectly melted.

"Right here, darling. Right here," he said as he tucked a handkerchief into this collar. Old school, I loved it.

"Yes, chief. Some are good. Some are successful. But what is success?" he asked as he took a bite of his enchilada. I sunk my teeth into the hot burrito waiting to hear his answer. "Not rhetorical. You answer. I'm eating."

"Success? Jeez. Having a goal and achieving it," I responded.

"Any goal? So taking out the trash?" he asked.

"Well, yeah I guess so," I said.

"So the same word is used for taking out the trash or starting a billion dollar company?" he asked. I raised my eyebrows, seeing his point. "Success can be many things. I subscribe to this: success is the progressive realization of a worthy ideal. All because someone is famous doesn't mean they're pointless or corrupt. That's crucial. Those that are in the spotlight, that truly love what they do, will always have a negative stigma. While we have our average celebrity gone awry, we also have a few good ones. Brad Pitt has donated millions to rebuild New Orleans, Angelina Jolie has built clean water systems for Somalia. And so on."

"And you were one of the first to fight racial injustice against blacks and Native Americans before it was fashionable to do so. And you refused to pick up an Oscar award in protest," I added. His face blushed as he finished off his enchilada and moved on to his rice and beans.

"Even aside from altruism," he said, "you have thespians like Daniel Day-Lewis that love their craft, and filmmakers like Martin Scorsese and Christopher Nolan that truly have a genuine passion for the art of filmmaking. We must be aware enough to realize that most of the famous are good, admirable people, equally as righteous and equally as earnest as your average car mechanic or Walmart greeter. Many did not necessarily seek fame and many of them don't use it badly. Just like how not all those on social media are chasing fame. To group them all in one basket is naïve and unjust. Not all those under the spotlight are there because their goal was to be seen. But many human beings today are running towards the spotlight for only that reason, when in reality they belong somewhere else where they would be much, much more accomplished.

"If you love acting, and I mean you would enjoy performing in front of your cat the same as you would in front of a Broadway audience, then acting is for you. It is noble. It is art. It is worthwhile, amazing, and brilliant. It is the best possible thing on the planet that you could be doing. This profession is no less and no more noble than being a teacher or a pediatrician, and no less down to earth than being a gas station owner or a computer programmer… if that is what you love doing and you are using it to do good. Use it… to do… good. Chasing your own dream, independent of any influence or fallacy, is the most captivating and congenial quest one can make. Remember that, chief."

He insisted on paying for dinner, and hurriedly walked back to his car, not wanting to stop for pictures or autographs. He gave me a bear hug and got back in his vehicle. He hopped in, started the engine, and rolled down his window. Sticking his head out, he smiled at me.

"Remember, chief. Success is the progressive realization of a worthy ideal. The ideal is yours to decide, and the realization is yours to pursue."

I. Ashmawey

18

Davenport

I. Ashmawey

Davenport

I f you were to ask me how I felt about my davenport sofa, I would tell you I liked it. I would have a fair share of things to say about it if I was asked. Let me tell you the story of my davenport sofa. It's worth hearing.

While in school, I knew that as soon as I graduated, I would need to find a place to live, and a sofa. I was, and always have been, the type that preferred to sleep on my couch. So a few months before graduation, as I was looking for one bedroom apartments or more affordable studio apartments, I simultaneously looked for sofas. I had only a handful of requirements:

1. That it was within my reach. This, of course, meant that it was affordable and attainable.
2. That it was comfortable. I had been used to a college dorm life for four years. I would be changing a lot already by living completely on my own. So I at least wanted something that would keep me comfortable.
3. That it was nice. I wanted something that if someone came to visit me, they'd say "Hey, that's a nice sofa." Especially since it would likely be the only piece of furniture I owned. So I wanted it to speak to who I was.

This sofa, in essence, would protect me and give me all I need. Dramatic? Not if you remember the first piece of furniture you ever bought.

I had been eyeing one particular sofa for months. I first saw it when I was walking through a massive and colossal Ikea store with a friend who was ready to take the leap on *his* first sofa. I personally wasn't thinking about that yet, I guess I was a late bloomer when it came to maturity. I was actually getting tired of walking in circles with him so I decided to head to their cafeteria for some famous Ikea chocolate cake. But on that fateful walk was when I saw my davenport.

Let me describe it to you. The color was the most astounding. It was blue, but it was also gray, depending on the light. It had a shine to it, giving it class. It was incredibly comfortable, oh so comfortable. And for your information, it would only become more comfortable over the years.

I. Ashmawey

Five years later, and I couldn't have been happier with my davenport. And with every passing day, more and more connections happened between me and my sofa. I wore it in, for one. It became more comfortable since, quite simply, I had sat in it more. I found my place in it, and it found its place in me. So every time I sat was more comfortable than the time before. Another connection that happened was the memories. The parties I've thrown on the sofa. The intimate conversations I've had on it. The memorable movies I've watched, books I've read, songs I've listened to, meals I've had on it. Therein grew a sense of mutual loyalty between man and material.

Why then, after all this, did I ever think of buying another sofa? How could I, after all I've said and expressed? The answer is: I had to. But arriving at that decision was the most difficult of my life to date. It started with a simple conversation I had with my fiancé, Bella.

"I wanna talk to you about your sofa," she said one night, as we laid on it after watching a movie together.

"Good old, davenport? What about her?" I asked.

"Don't take this the wrong way, but it's time you got a new one."

"What!?" I screamed at her. "Have you lost your mind? Why on earth would I want another one? Better question, what's wrong with this one that I would even look for another one?" I asked.

"What's wrong with this one? Have you forgotten your complaints to me? Every cushion is torn. It's so worn down that it's not even comfortable anymore. It's starting to smell, you're the one who noticed that. People come over and are grossed out by it, it's literally ruining your social life. When you look at it, you're not even happy. So… what do you mean 'what's wrong with this one'?" she asked. I froze with my mouth hung open. She was right. It's amazing how much a person doesn't listen to their own complaints. They can even entirely forget they ever made them, which is what happened.

"Okay, that may be true," I started. "But think of it this way, in a couple of years, it will have been ten years of one couch and that would financially be an amazing thing. That's a great savings and I don't want to give that up."

"Sure, that's fine. Or, maybe you move on to another couch now, and your entire life changes. How about that? Maybe a new couch would somehow give you a better standard of living and better relationships and better income," Bella said. "What if you're just scared?"

Scared.

Was I scared? I wasn't scared. Scared of what? Of buying a new couch?

"I'm not scared to buy a new couch," I said. What an absurd accusation.

"No, you're scared of leaving this one. If you could have both, you would. But you don't have enough room, no one has two couches," Bella responded. I got up from my davenport and looked at it. I saw the holes, the tears. I smelled the stench. It had gotten old. Maybe it was good to me a while back, maybe only for a bit. And I've spent years cleaning it, treating it well. I felt like, at the end of the day, I had given more to my davenport than it had given to me. Maybe it was time to stop giving it and instead get a new one? Then I closed my eyes… and I remembered the good times. All the laughs and comfort it had provided me over the years.

No. No, I wasn't going to do this.

"Bella, I don't know what stake you have in this, but you're ruining this for me. Get out."

"What?" she asked.

"Please, get out. I'm happy," I said solemnly. And she did, confused.

Later that night, I couldn't sleep. Had I wronged Bella? No, I didn't think so, but I also didn't care. Instead, I thought of one thing: was it time to get a new sofa? Then something strange happened. Out of nowhere, and completely subconsciously, I remembered every bad thing that ever happened to me because of my sofa. Everything, from the ruined dates to the canceled parties, from the insects that made homes inside the torn holes to the cricks in my back from the uncomfortable evenings I've had on it. It was horrible. Why was I ever okay with this? Why hadn't I moved on sooner?

Because I was scared.

I had the world at my fingertips. I could have the best life ever, everything I ever wanted. And I wasn't going after it because of one thing: I was scared. What an utter waste. After those thoughts, I felt empowered. I needed that, it was my catharsis. I needed to remember all the bad things that happened in order to make the right decision. After that, I didn't hesitate. After that, I didn't look back or question my decision. It was done.

I picked up my phone and called Bella.

"Hello?" she said.

"Bella, will you come with me tomorrow to buy a new sofa?" I asked.

Silence. Then…

"I would absolutely love to," she said.

"Thank you. Goodnight." And with that, I hung up. Laying on my back, on my old davenport, I closed my eyes. And I already knew, my life was going to be better.

I. Ashmawey

19

Dreams of the Wildest

I. Ashmawey

"I've been Dean of this department for over twenty-seven years. Six of which, I've been on tenure," Dean Maxwell Vintage spoke with furrowed eyebrows. He sat back in his leather chair behind his colossal, mahogany desk. His hands in front of his chest, tips of fingers touching those of the opposite hand. He looked at Professor Darling Wilson under crooked eyebrows. "And in all these years, I've yet to come across a study that I have... expostulated... as much as yours."

Darling didn't shift in her seat, she didn't waver in resolution, and the subtle smile on her face only became less subtle. She did not have any anger towards Dean Vintage at all. Not in the slightest. But Darling was the kind of woman who only became stronger in the face of adversity. In fact, she tried to hide her growing smile but visibly failed.

"Dr. Wilson," Dean Vintage continued, "I can even go as far as saying that your study is not founded in any scientific approach whatsoever." The Dean was clearly angry and wanted to elicit anger in his inferior. Something surprisingly immature and unbefitting of the Dean of Psychology at one of the most respected universities in the country.

"Dean Vintage," Darling began, "You know very well how much I respect your knowledge and opinions, sir. This project, however, I feel very strongly about." Maxwell Vintage shook his head as she talked, and shook it harder when she finished talking. There was no use. "Dean..."

"No, forget it, Darling," he interrupted her. "Forget it. I care about your future, and it pains me to stand idly and watch you throw it away. But I can't force sense into you." All of a sudden, a much more fatherly side to him appeared. He had been working with Darling for almost a decade now. She was like a career daughter to him and he saw so much incredible potential in her.

"Dean," she closed her eyes, channeling the other side to her as well. "I understand that you only care about my future. The university will be fine, whether or not I release a bogus study. I understand. But my future—"

"Will be ruined."

"Yes, I understand that. Sir, my daughter Cindy..."

"I know what your daughter's name is, Darling," he reminded her. She smiled.

"I know," she responded. "Anyway, as you also know, she's only five. Now, lately, she's been having a similar dream over and over. She describes it to me in such vivid detail. A huge oak tree at the top of a small hill with a branch so strong that she can climb and lay on. Daffodils around the tree reaching all the way to a rushing creek a few yards away. She lays on the branch for hours listening to the water, reading books, and sleeping. She's had this dream over and over, but it's never exactly the same. She does different things every time."

"Darling," he spoke in a deep voice. "She's a child. And she dreams of sitting in a garden doing nothing. That's hardly a reason to conduct a study on dreams. All I'm saying is this: be prepared for the worst when this is over. You'll have to explain to my superiors why you wasted years on this."

"I understand, Dean," she gave up. "I understand. It's okay, sir. Hopefully, I can always start over with something better afterward if this ends up being a waste of time."

And so it was that the last person she had hopes in believing in her, did not. She left his office without an ounce of remission, however. She believed in this project, and it would only be a matter of hours before all her data would be analyzed. She walked across campus back to her office. The sun was shining strong and the happy voices of people out and about made her think of how much she couldn't wait for nighttime. For it was during the night that people dreamed, and that's what she needed.

Her cell phone rang, it was her husband.

"Hi, honey," she said.

"Hey, beautiful. I just picked Cindy up and we're heading to the park for a bit. Any chance you can join us?" he asked.

"No, honey. I'm sorry," she responded. "It's going to be a long night for me. The results come out tonight and I have to be here when they do."

"Yeah, I understand. We'll be fine though," he said.

"Let me talk to Cindy for a second," she said. She heard the phone being transferred to her daughter.

"Hi, mommy."

"Hi, my princess! I miss you. Honey, did you have any dreams last night?" she asked.

"Yes, mommy."

"The same dream, honey?" Darling asked.

"Yes, mommy. And you were there too!"

"... I was?"

"Yes, we were reading together," Cindy said. Darling thought about that. She needed to put that into the data.

"Okay, honey. I'll see you later tonight, baby. Bye."

Darling got to her office and checked the status of the analysis: 84% complete. Data on over 300 million dreams, all being analyzed in the most excruciating detail. 300 million dreams from 300 million different people from all around the world being fed into one massive program that had taken ten years to create. And analyzing all these dreams for one thing and one thing only: the location of the dream. Where exactly was the dream taking place? Not when, not the day, not the time of year. Just where.

Darling plopped herself on her comfortable leather desk chair and rolled over to her computer. She had quite a while to wait. But in the meantime, she would study the data so far. She had been spot checking different dreams from different geographical regions, trying to see if there was a connection. Her desk phone rang.

"This is Dr. Wilson."

"Dr. Wilson. This is Dr. James Leigh from the Physics Department." The Physics Department? What was this about?

"Okay," she responded questioningly.

"I've been hearing a lot about your project, Dr. Wilson. Your study. I myself have been conducting some research and I think some of our research may overlap. Or at least complement the other."

"How so?"

"Well, I study multiverses," he said. Oh great, a nutcase. But any more of a nutcase than she was? "Parallel universes, Dr. Wilson. I've been studying astral projection, that's the traveling of the consciousness from the body to other realities."

"So far, I'm not hearing much overlap, Doctor," she said. She realized afterward that it sounded a bit rude.

"Doctor, what I am implying is this. What if during the state of dreaming, one travels to different parallel realities?" he asked. Parallel realities? She had not thought of that. She was currently analyzing the data and yes, she was hoping to find some common themes between people's dreams, but parallel realities? "Would you be available tomorrow to meet?"

"Yes," she responded.

"Great, let's meet for lunch at the cafeteria," he said. And they hung up. As much as she wanted to delve into this possibility in research and thought, she couldn't. Not now. Not only because she was expecting results soon and needed to clear her mind for it, but because she was incredibly tired. She shut her eyes for a moment. So much was happening now.

Suddenly, she was on a hilltop. An oak tree, with daffodils all around it. And a creek nearby with flowing water. The sights, the sounds, everything. She looked up, and there she was. Cindy, sleeping on the bulky branch. Darling stood there, smiling, with a tear forming at the corner of her eye. She was there, and she was aware of it. And it was beautiful.

The buzzer woke her up. The results were finished. It took Darling a few seconds to remember where she was, she was not in the dream with her daughter. She looked at the results, and she couldn't believe her eyes.

Out of over 300 million dreams, from 300 million different people from all around the world, there we ninety-nine distinct locations that people dreamt about. That only meant one thing, and one thing only, and it was further confirmed by what she heard from Dr. Leigh.

Darling rested her head on her chair once again, closed her eyes, and traveled back again to where her daughter was, to read her a book in the oak tree.

20

Eye of the Visiting Beholders

The aliens landed on New Year's Eve in London, England. Right in the middle of Piccadilly Circus, in front of thousands of people flooding the streets and many, many more watching at home. We eventually learned they were peaceful, though of course, our race did not believe so at first. Nine years passed since they arrived. In that time, so much had happened.

First were the wars. Not between us and the aliens—who were called Ertugs—but amongst ourselves. Half the world's population wanted to attack the Ertugs upon their arrival, the other half wanted to attempt communication. And so, a worldwide civil war erupted, all while the Ertugs hovered a few miles above the Earth's surface in their spacecrafts, watching, waiting. Interestingly, the civil war allowed for everyone's hidden biases and hatred to appear. Countries began killing each other because of long buried animosity that had nothing to do with the aliens.

Thankfully, the side that wanted to connect with the Ertugs prevailed. Not to play down the number of deaths that finally allowed that happen. The countries were still divided, but at least there was a coalition and a Council of Representatives. Nine years after the Ertugs' arrival, we were finally ready to communicate with them.

All the meanwhile, they had been watching, waiting. As one may imagine, the first thing the Ertugs wanted to discuss was the nine-year war they witnessed from start to finish. Naively, and quite embarrassingly, the Council wanted to act like it hadn't happened. When they saw it didn't work, they at least attempted to downplay it as if it were minor.

The Ertugs communicated to us telepathically. There was no evidence they were able to read minds, only send communication. The Ertugs were also shape-shifters. So when they appeared to humans, they appeared in human form except for one main difference, they were colorless. They were not see through, but rather a reflective chrome color like liquid mercury. However, once we realized they communicated to us telepathically, we began wondering whether they had truly shape-shifted to human form or just convinced us that they did.

After a few months of introductory meetings, and after it was established there would be no hostility from either species to the other, the Council allowed for future sessions with the Ertugs to be internationally broadcast. The meetings were simple—held in the Palace of Westminster—one delegate was appointed from each side to represent each race. They sat casually at a round, wooden table with two comfortable green fabric chairs. The room was a basic interrogation style room surrounded with one-way mirrors from every direction. The public was not briefed on the details of the prior conversations.

From the human race, Dr. Harrison Burridge, professor of sociology and prolific writer in his field, was chosen. Some thought him an unusual choice; most assumed the Council would appoint someone of a more political nature. Rather, it chose a man whose general opinions few disagreed with. A man who's insight into the human race made him an ideal candidate for the position. And as far as the public knew, he had been doing a great job. From the Ertugs, a member of the expedition named Selchan was chosen. He was the expedition chef. As one would expect, the Council was most confused when they learned of Selchan's profession. Why would a chef be the best choice to speak to a foreign species? Surely there was a captain. Would they not be a more logical choice?

The representatives of the species approached each other with smiles, perfectly mimicking each other, and sat at the table. After the applause and introductions, and after the establishing of the format of the meeting, they finally began. Selchan asked the first question.

"Dr. Harrison Burridge," Selchan spoke telepathically. Right off the bat, what astonished all humans was that there was no physical or geographical limit to the Ertugs telepathy. All those who desired to hear Selchan speak, did; even if they were thousands of miles away and Selchan—as much as they knew—was not aware of them. And those who did not desire to hear Selchan, did not. He sounded of a calm male voice, not too deep and not a hint of hoarseness. "Does your species have a creator?"

Dr. Burridge cleared his throat before beginning. "Many believe we do. Many believe we do not. What about you? Does your kind have one?"

"It is the same. Most believe we do. Some few do not," Selchan responded. "Do you believe your Creator asks you to fight?"

"No, quite the opposite. All accounts of the Creator state rather explicitly not to fight," Burridge responded. "He desires us, as most of us desire, to be good to each other. How about you? For those who believe in your Creator, what do you believe he desires of you?"

"To live purposefully. And for those who do not, they are tested," Selchan said. This piqued Burridge's interest.

"Tested how?"

"Why do you fight each other?" Selchan asked.

"Because we fear what is different. Why did you not answer my last question?" Burridge asked.

"Because if you do not know the answer, I cannot give it to you," Selchan responded. "You said you fear what is different. So what do you fear? And why does that cause you to fight?"

"Well, we fear each other. And we fight each other because we are different from one another," Burridge explained. This was met with a short pause before Selchan spoke again.

"Do you mean different, as in you are all unique individuals?" Selchan asked.

"No, not different in individuality. Rather different in race. Skin color, for example, has been one of the primary reasons that we humans have fought and treated each other with such horror in the past." This was again met with another pause.

"What is skin color?" Selchan asked. This question was not taken well. Spectators were visibly annoyed. It felt like the questions were becoming less interesting and more elementary.

"Well, skin! It's what we have covering our external bodies. And it comes in different colors. It's one of the ways we differ from one another."

Selchan stood up. "We shall continue tomorrow. I must confer with my delegation," Selchan said. A bit taken back, Burridge stood up to bid him farewell for the day. Selchan paused on his way out. "I'm sorry. Dr. Burridge, I have one more question."

"Yes, Selchan?"

"How do you know that what you are seeing is the same as everyone else?" Selchan asked.

"Well," Dr. Burridge scratched his head. This was a philosophical question. "I suppose you can say we use verification. If I see a flower as red, and I tell you that I do, and you confirm that you also see it as red, then we have verified it."

"What if red looks different to the two of us?" Selchan asked, still standing. "What if my red is your green? We would never know, would we?" Harrison Burridge just stared at him, not knowing what to say. He slightly shook his head, and then Selchan spoke again. "Have a good day." And then he left.

The public response was not a good one. People wondered why the Ertug, Selchan, seemed so obtuse. Especially when the initial thought was this was a superior race. Superior? Superior in what? Clearly, Selchan was not very bright. Perhaps the problem here was hiring the chef to communicate.

The next day, the two sat at the same table once again. And once again, all eyes were on them. Two different beings joining together to witness cross-species communication. And, as with the day before, Selchan was the first to speak.

"I apologize for my abrupt departure. I needed to consult with my delegation," Selchan said.

"That's quite alright," Burridge said.

"Dr. Burridge. It is our belief that you are unaware of who you are."

"Oh, is that right? How so?" Burridge asked. Already, he felt today would not be any better than the day before.

"Till now, we have communicated with your species telepathically. And this communication has only been audible. After consulting with my delegation, we have decided that we must progress to the next level of communication: visual telepathy. Dr. Harrison Burridge, I shall communicate with you, and all those who wish to receive my communication, using visual telepathy."

"Selchan, what will you communicate?" Burridge asked. His voice had a hint of hesitation. Perhaps even fear.

"What I see."

"Why would you communicate to us what you see?" Burridge asked.

"We believe it may be an interesting insight for you," Selchan explained. Then, in the blink of an eye, all those watching closed their eyes simultaneously. And then they saw. Not in their minds, as in cognitive thoughts, but they actually saw. Behind their eyelids, they saw exactly what Selchan was seeing. And what he was seeing, they did not understand. They saw Harrison Burridge, as Selchan himself looked: a chrome, reflective color.

Burridge opened his eyes. "Why do you see me like this?"

"We see all of you the way you are. The question is, why do you see yourselves, and each other, differently?"

"You are seeing all of us like this?" Burridge asked. His heart rate was now faster.

"You don't understand," Selchan said. "This is who you are. But it seems your Creator was… testing you. And apparently, you have failed so miserably."

Burridge stood up so suddenly that his chair fell back, hitting the ground. He looked in the one-way mirror in front of him, and there he was, colorless. The way he was created. The way all humanity looked. And the way he would see all people for the rest of his life.

21

Star Trek Displacement

I n an open, rocky desert, cruel with heat, William Shatner, Leonard Nimoy, and DeForest Kelley suddenly materialize. Literally appearing out of thin air. With no civilization in sight, they look around and see nothing.

"What in God's name..." Shatner says. "Are you guys okay?"

"Where in heaven's name are we, Bill?" DeForest asks, looking around. "Weren't we just on set? Did I have a bit too much to drink during lunch?"

"No. No, your drink was soft, Kelley. I lied to you," William responds. "But... I could swear... okay, I have no idea what's happening. Something isn't right."

"Guys," Leonard interjects. "I suggest we concentrate on our current location. Perhaps that in itself will answer some questions."

"But I see nothing around us!" William says, looking around. "No people. No cars. No civilization! I don't know. Something doesn't feel right, guys."

"A gut feeling, Bill?" Leonard asks.

"More than that. It's intuition," DeForest explains. "When something doesn't feel right, it isn't *only* be a feeling."

"On the contrary," Leonard says. "A feeling is exactly what it would be, a feeling. As you so eloquently just stated."

William smiles at them both. "You're sounding a lot like your characters. You know that?"

"Perhaps we should... just begin walking. Standing here most certainly won't get us anywhere," Leonard says. William nods affirmatively, when he notices something shiny in the sand. A glistening sparkle. He reaches for it and brushes sand off with the tips of his fingers. He pulls out a soda can.

"Pepsi, huh? Looks a bit... different," William exclaims. He turns the can over and reads the bottom. "Expiration. December first... two-thousand and eighteen!" He drops the can to the ground.

"Most peculiar," Leonard says, slightly above a whisper. The trio stands desolately in awe at the newly found information.

"How could this happen?" DeForest asks with fervor in his voice.

I. Ashmawey

"Explanation, Leonard?" William asks.

"Unknown. The longevity of soda can is roughly six to nine months. So, what I can surmise is that we are clearly in the Earth date two-thousand eighteen."

William thinks to himself for a minute, pacing on the sandy dirt. "We need to make contact with the studio immediately. Explain to them the situation. We were in the studio when this happened. So maybe they'll have record of our disappearance and have some way to help us get back to our time. So, I guess we should start moving. I'm sure we'll get to a city within a few miles."

"A few miles," Leonard says. "Well, it could have been worse."

"Sure," DeForest says, rolling his eyes. "Two miles in the desert, in the past, with an optimistic dictator and a robotic supporter. Could have been worse."

"I sense you are being sarcastic, DeForest," Leonard says. "But your odds of survival are greatly increased by the fact that you have a sanguine leader and myself." DeForest walks off, mumbling something under his breath that sounded like, *Don't bet on it.* But Leonard couldn't tell for sure.

Arriving at a small town an hour later, the three musketeers are astounded as they look around. William, being the natural leader, still knows what's important. At the first street bench they come across, he finds a winter hat lying unattended. He grabs it and gives it to Leonard who puts it on.

"You can't take those ears off, huh?" William asks. Leonard shakes his head.

"No. Only the makeup artists can," Leonard responds.

"We need to contact the studio before anything else," William tells Leonard.

"Well, we have no idea where to get our hands on a phone in this age. They probably don't even have phones," DeForest adds angrily.

"You are most correct, Kelley. Which makes me think that we may have to resort to a more folk method of attaining research," Leonard adds.

"Well, what's that?" DeForest asks.

"We ascertain the data that we need by verbally probing the surrounding humans."

"You mean... we ask people?" DeForest asks.

"Colloquially expressed. Though, accurate," Leonard says. William looks at them both like they're insane.

"How about I go speak to someone? Okay? Wait here and... try to blend in," William says strangely. He leaves them and walks across the street trying to find someone to talk to. Sitting on a bench is an elderly woman with dark sunglasses and a brand name purse. "Excuse me, ma'am. Do you happen to know where the office of Desilu studio is?"

"The who?" she asks.

"Desilu, ma'am. You know, I Love Lucy?"

"You're a bit late on that, sonny. Got get yourself a star map and see who's

138

around today." She gets up and walks away slowly.

"What's a star map?" William asks to himself. He asks another person and gets a similar reaction.

Back with Leonard and DeForest, the two try to get over why everything on the planet looks so different than how they expected the future to look.

"We don't have flying vehicles by twenty-eighteen?" DeForest wonders.

"Sustained, anti-gravity elevation... we really should by now."

"Thank you, Leonard," DeForest says to Leonard, who doesn't hear him. He observes a teenage girl taking a selfie with her phone, then taking another, then another. After each snap, she checks her phone to see how it turned out.

"Very interesting," Leonard says.

"What's that?"

"There's something. Compact, palm-sized computers." The two look around and see everyone in the street staring at their cell phones. On the opposite sidewalk, two men walk towards each other, both looking at their phones. They soon collide, exchange a quick "sorry", then go back to how they were.

DeForest looks to Leonard and faux laughs. "Well, maybe they're research-ing something important. Can you go peek and see what they're all doing with those computers?" Leonard gets up and slyly walks behind a few girls. He looks over their shoulders for a few minutes with a puzzled look on his face. He comes back to DeForest.

"It looks like they are socializing with each other... through the computers. Searching for celebrity news and sport games. And something called Kardashian. Fas-cinating. It seems that technology in the future has evolved so quickly, much faster than in our time. But other aspects haven't evolved."

"What do you mean, Leonard?"

"It seems that we have evolved in the most... useless of fashions."

"Colloquially expressed, Leonard," DeForest jabs. At the same moment, William comes up to them with a perplexed look on his face. "How did it go, Bill?"

"People are... ruder than I anticipated," William says.

"William," Leonard says, "evidence so far shows confirms that the future is far from what we predicted in our time."

"Well, what info do you have?" William asks.

"We don't have enough," Leonard responds. "We've only gathered bits and pieces, but we need more.

"Well," William says, "there's only one place to go in any civilized society when you need access to large amounts of information."

A few minutes later, the three enter the city library. They immediately notice it's not very well kept. "Not as updated as I expected. Nonetheless, information is information. Can you work these computers, Leonard?"

I. Ashmawey

"I shall certainly try," Leonard sits at one of the computers in the middle of the library floor. William and DeForest look around and then to each other.

"It's so… empty," William says.

"Maybe society has already intellectually evolved enough."

"Doubtful," William says. "But more importantly, when is it ever enough?"

"Guys?" Leonard calls out William and DeForest. They join him at the computer. "I was able to pull some information and got a summary of the current year. Here's a highlight of things so far." Leonard hits a few buttons and plays a slideshow on the computer that shows murders, homicides, suicides, terrorism, bullying, and police brutality. The number of deaths, the amount of domestic violence, the amount of political violence, it's all too much to handle. The three watch in shock.

"This can't be Earth," William says under his breath. "It can't be who we will become."

"It's barbaric," DeForest says.

"No. Even the most barbaric times in Earth's history were better than this," William says. It's like people have lost all sense of humanity. How can a society become so desensitized to death? Like it's a game or something." William runs his fingers through his hair, eyes spread wide.

"I don't get it, Bill. What are these people missing?" DeForest asks.

"They're missing the main ingredient for evolution," William says. "People evolve when they realize the value of each individual human life. This society doesn't see that. Parents killing their children. Law enforcement killing innocents, and then retaliation. Terrorist groups spewing ignorance and violence. Government officials perpetuating hate. It's like everyone is degenerating and the only response people have made is to degenerate even further! And no one wants to stop the cycle."

"It is rather disconcerting," Leonard says, eyes still fixated on the screen.

"There must have been a glitch in the timeline somehow," William says, with a glisten of hope in his voice. "This twenty-eighteen is clearly different than anything we ever expected. The only explanation is that something happened between our present and this future that had massive effects."

"Agreed, William," Leonard says.

"Well, what do we do now?" DeForest asks.

"We'll figure it out," William quickly responds. "Let's get out of here, though. There's nothing here for us."

Outside the library, walking in the back alleyway, two policemen stop them.

"Hey!" the first policeman says. "Stop right there."

"Can we help you, officers?" William asks.

The second policeman approaches them. "We've gotten a few reports about three strange-looking men."

William chuckles. "Well, sirs, that cannot be us. We were just catching up on some reading in there."

"Hey! Keep your hands where I can see them!" the first policeman yells out.

"Relax," the second policeman says. "No one's accusing you of anything. We're just going to ask you a few questions."

The first policeman points at Leonard. "Hey! You! I told you to keep your hands where I can see them. Now take off your hat!"

"Sir, I—" Leonard hesitates.

"Take your hat off!" the same policeman repeats. Hesitantly, Leonard removes his hat and his prop ears are revealed.

"What in the hell?!" the first policeman yells out.

"Officers!" William tries to intervene. "Allow me to explain!"

"Sir!" Leonard says. "It's just makeup. I am no different than any of—" But in that second, the first policeman fires his gun and hits Leonard directly in the in his shoulder. Leonard violently hits the brick wall in the alley and falls to the ground. The second policeman pauses in shock, while the first one stands his ground. DeForest runs to Leonard. The second policeman turns around and calls an ambulance.

"Try not to move, Leonard," DeForest says as he tries to stop the bleeding.

"What is this nightmare?" William asks.

"Bill…" Leonard starts.

"Don't talk!" DeForest yells. "You need to conserve your energy."

"You must allow me to speak," Leonard insists. "I don't think we only traveled through time. I think it was a rip in the continuum, a parallel universe. While we did additionally travel through time, this is the not the twenty-eighteen of our reality." Just then, three men come into the alley, dressed in black and wearing dark sunglasses.

"Gentlemen, Desilu Productions," one of the men says. He then taps each of the policemen on the back, and the policemen freeze in place. They become entirely paralyzed, like they're in a form of stasis. "We have a lot to explain to you. But we can take you back to your time now."

"Holy catfish," William says. "How'd you guys do this?"

"It's a new initiative that we have in the future. Your future. It helps our actors get in character better. But, as you can see, we've had some issues," one of the men in black says.

"Okay, whatever. Take us the hell back and we'll discuss this later."

"William," Leonard says. "I wish to stay."

"What!?" DeForest says. "Are you out of your mind?"

"Mr. Nimoy," one of the men in black says, "that cannot happen."

"Bill," Leonard starts. "This Earth. This reality. It will not survive without evolving. And it will not evolve without my help."

I. Ashmawey

"That is not your responsibility," William responds. "We don't interfere. You of all people Leonard... of *all* people, you know this best!"

"A policeman shot you, Leonard," DeForest reminds him. "That's a pretty sure sign that a society is hopeless. He was angry, and so he shot you. That's a world you want to save?"

"Anger is not a real emotion, DeForest," Leonard responds. "His emotion was fear. He feared me because he did not know me. Fear, confusion, and yes, hate. He hated me without even knowing me."

"Leonard, he tried to kill you!" DeForest says.

"Leonard," William says. "I understand what you're saying. But this world... they've lost all sight of what is possible. If you told them they can live in a place with no violence, they'd only laugh at you. They'd never believe that's a possibility."

"He's right, Leonard. You said it yourself, they only progress in useless things. And they'll never have what we hope for our future. Instead of looking up to the stars, they look down to their devices."

"I know," Leonard says. "But someone has to break the cycle. I will not hide who I am. I will join them. If that policemen won't approach me to get to know me, I will approach him. And when he knows me, he will not fear me anymore."

"Mr. Nimoy," one of the men in black says, "we are sorry. We really are. Your sense of duty is commendable. But you're traveling back with us." The men in black take out a small device from one of their pockets and hit a button. Lights begin shining and the five men's bodies began to disintegrate. In the last second, Leonard steps out of his beam. William sees that and reaches his hand out, but is too late.

"Leonard!" The rest of the men disappear, and Leonard stands alone.

"Live long, and prosper, my friends." Leonard grabs his hat and throws it to the ground. He leaves the alley, returning back to the people.

22

The Touching Adventure

I. Ashmawey

G randpa Joe rocked forward and backward in his solid, oak rocking chair, comfortably nestled in the family room. Forward, and backward, and forward again. On the couch next to him was his seven-year-old grandson, Sam. His eyes were covered with virtual reality gear and on the TV, he projected what he saw. On the other end of the couch, sat Sam's thirteen-year-old sister, Zoe. With earpieces dug deep into her ear canal, she moved her thumbs at phenomenal speeds, typing away on her phone.

Forward, backward, and forward again, Grandpa Joe rocked. "I'm going to go on an adventure," he said.

"What game? And on what console?" Sam asked, eyes still covered, as he held controllers in both hands. He was deeply engaged in fighting his virtual war.

"No, no game. I'm going to go on a real adventure," Grandpa Joe said.

"I don't understand, Grandpa," Sam said. "What makes it real?"

"Sam, I'm going outside for an adventure. Are you going to join me?"

"I can't right now, Grandpa," Sam responded. "I'm just about to break into the secret base."

Grandpa Joe looked over to Zoe. "Zoe," he called out. No response, her fingers moved faster than ever, tippity tapping on her phone. "Zoe?" Nothing. She didn't even raise her eyes from her phone. "Very well. That's fine you two." Grandpa got up from his rocking chair, took a moment to straighten his back, then slowly dragged his feet across the floor towards the front door.

Stepping out into the sunlight, he took a good look around. He was old and didn't have as much energy as he once did. In the backyard, there was a small pond surrounded by a garden. And overlooking the scenery, there was one lonely bench. Perhaps, if Grandpa Joe could make his way to the bench, he'd take a seat and rest a bit. And so he did. At the very least, he was happy to be out in the sun and enjoying the fresh air.

And so, he sat, and thought about his grandchildren. Would they ever experience any real adventures? Adventures with real, live in flesh, human beings? Or at the very least, honest inanimate objects! An actual thing they can hold in their hands, or heck, just experience with their sense of touch. He was fully aware he wasn't necessarily having an adventure in that moment. At least not yet.

That changed when he heard a voice coming from beneath the bench he sat on.

"Can you help us?" the voice asked. It was a soft feminine voice, but sounded incredibly small. *At least some children still played outside*, he thought.

"Who's speaking?" Grandpa Joe asked.

"Down here please," the voice said again.

"Down? Under the bench?" Grandpa Joe asked. "Why, I can't bend down that far. If you'll please make yourself visible." After a moment of silence, he heard some ruffling of grass and leaves. The children had decided to come out.

Except they weren't children. They had the shape of humans, but they were the size of Grandpa Joe's palm! "Good God!" he gasped. "What are you?!"

"We're trolls," the little girl said, the one who had spoken before. "You shouldn't fear us. It's us who are afraid." There were three of them; this girl, and two boys. They were dressed in pilgrim clothes and had pale, white faces with straight, black hair. "My name is Bixby. These are my brothers, Venjo, and Zenjo."

A few moments later, at least it felt like a few, Grandpa Joe opened his eyes to find himself lying on his back on the bench. And upon opening them, he saw Bixby standing on his chest, looking down at him.

"Oh good, you're awake now," she said with a smile. She adjusted her bonnet and jumped off of him. "You fainted, sir."

Grandpa Joe slowly sat himself up. He looked around, not a person in sight. "What are..."

"We're trolls. We already told you," Venjo said. The three were barely visible as they stood on the bench.

"Hush, Venjo," Bixby said. "Sir, what are you called?"

"Called? Why, I'm Grandpa Joe," he said with pride.

"Grandpa Joe," Bixby said. "With due respect, we can spend time telling you where we came from, where we live now, how it is that we ended up here, all that. Or, you can help us as we are in dire need of it."

Grandpa Joe didn't need to think, not for a second. He hadn't a clue what was going on and he was pretty sure he had knocked his head, got a concussion, and these were all hallucinations. But darn it, he was fine with that.

"Yes. Yes, Bixby. I'll help you."

Bixby looked to Venjo and Zenjo with a smile. They nodded back. "Thank you, Grandpa Joe," she said. He smiled at them, what a day this has been. "Now please kill the sea serpent."

"What in tarnations did you say?" Grandpa Joe asked. Even for a hallucination, that was a bit intense. "A sea serpent? Where is there a sea serpent and why would I kill it?"

"It's destroyed our homes, killed our kin, and threatens our very existence. And all for the most selfish and vile of reasons, mind you," Venjo said.

"It's a horrible creature. And only you can save us from it," Zenjo added. Grandpa Joe had never been involved in a fight in all his life. Not even as a young boy in school. As an adult, he never joined the army and never once even got in a scuffle. It's not that he wasn't brave, not at all. It's that he didn't know whether or not he was.

"Well…" Grandpa Joe hesitated. "What do I kill it with?" Just then, Bixby jumped down from the bench to the grass below. Above a patch of lawn, she moved her hands in a rhythmic fashion and conjured up an amazing sword, three feet in length. The silver handle had a red ruby right at the tip. "Outstanding," Grandpa Joe gasped.

"It's too heavy for me. Will you please pick it up?" Bixby asked. And so Grandpa Joe did. Suddenly he felt a surge of strength explode within him. An invigorating power he had never experienced before, not even during his glistening prime. He held the sword up to the sky and looked to the sun. He was strong, the strongest. Nothing could defeat him in that moment. "All you must do," Bixby started, "is call to the sea serpent. Say 'Oh you who lurks beneath water, reveal yourself to those above'."

And so, feeling like a young man ready to take on the world, Grandpa Joe screamed those words into the sky. In that same moment, a fountain spurt from the middle of the pond. The fountain got bigger and stronger, four feet above the surface of the water, five, six. Then from beneath the fountain came the snout of what seemed to be a dragon with a long, long… long neck. In fact, the more the creature came out, the more it was just neck. A sea serpent. Long, with a green, scaley, snake-like body with many fins sticking out randomly.

Grandpa Joe killed the hesitation inside him. As the serpent rose higher and higher, seven feet, eight, nine, and as he heard the trolls screaming and yelling, Grandpa Joe decided he wouldn't wait one more minute. He threw the sword with all the strength he had been saving his entire life. He aimed right for where he believed would be the serpent's heart, and it was a direct hit. The sea serpent let out a scream and much of its body went back into the water. Its head and only the top of it's neck fell onto the grass at the edge of the pond.

"Hooray!" Bixby screamed. "You did it!"

"Stupid sea serpent. Now we'll be able to use its body as a home," Venjo said.

"Wait, what?" Grandpa Joe screamed.

"Oh, yes," Zenjo said. "Sorry, pops. The sea serpent didn't actually do anything to us. But we wanted a bigger house. And we figured if we could kill the sea serpent, we can use its body as a home."

Grandpa Joe's heart began beating strongly. "Wha... how could you? That's barbaric."

"Sorry, Grandpa. But you played your part tremendously," Bixby said with a laugh. The three trolls went laughing away, dancing around the pond, waiting for the sea serpent to breathe its last breath. Grandpa Joe watched them scurry along as he dropped the sword to the ground. He looked to the sea serpent, breathing heavily with its head resting on the grass. He reluctantly got closer to it, inching forward.

"Sea serpent?" he said.

"I... will not... hurt you," the sea serpent said, labored. It's voice was deeper than the earth. "You may come closer."

"I'm so sorry, sea serpent," Grandpa Joe said. "Please, forgive me."

"You did not know. But only because you did not ask," the sea serpent said.

Grandpa Joe nodded his head. "Yes, yes you're right. I heard the trolls only, and did not think twice." A tear formed in his eye. "I'm so sorry. Is there anything I can do?"

"There is," the sea serpent said. "Your touch. A human touch can cure me." Grandpa Joe hesitated. He looked at the wound on the serpent's skin and looked at his hand. Even with what he had seen from the trolls, he still had difficulty trusting this creature. "Do not fear." And so Grandpa Joe did not. He got closer to the serpent and touched his hand to its wound. And like magic, as if everything he had seen that day was not magical enough, the wound disappeared. The sea serpent took a deep breath and lifted its head. "Thank you. Thank you, dearly." And within a second, its long neck-body slipped back into the water.

Grandpa Joe looked around, the trolls were gone as well. And the sword had vanished. Grandpa Joe stood in the backyard, by himself. After a few moments, he slowly made his way back to the house, opened the door, and stepped back inside. Walking into the family room, he saw his grandchildren just as he had left them. He sat down on the rocking chair and rocked forward, and backward, and forward again.

"What kind of adventure do you want to have?" Sam asked, still with the virtual reality gear on his eyes.

"Adventure?" Grandpa Joe asked, looking at Zoe, still working her thumbs away on her phone. "An adventure with a human touch."

23

For the Infinitesimal Affair

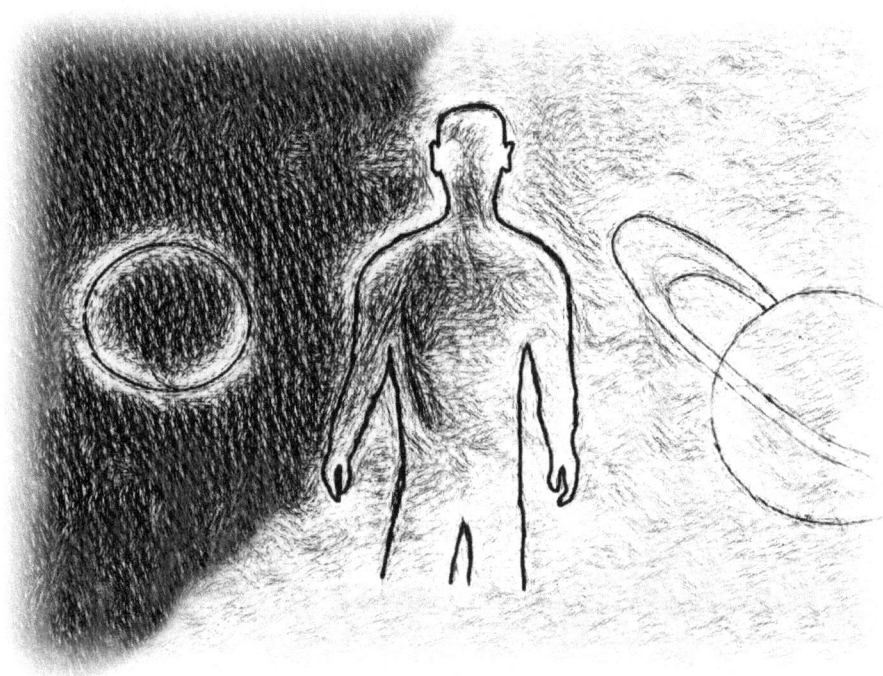

Monstrous, immeasurable, towering giants. In everything but size, their bodies perfectly resembled the human form. They wore one-piece uniforms, whiter than snow. Bald, not a single hair on their heads or faces. But massive, oh so massive. Our entire planet could easily fit in one of their palms. The day they came, was the day our world fell apart. Everything we knew—we thought we knew—was thrown out the window. Three of them came into our galaxy, walking giants through the universe. When they walked, we couldn't even see where their feet landed. Were they flying, or was there actually a ground beneath? We didn't know, and little did we care. We cared about them blocking our sun, or blowing it out simply by passing next to it. We cared about them stepping on us, or flicking our planet across the cosmos for fun.

There was no question that it was the end of times. For all the scientific progression we had made, all the political strength we had built, and all the wealth we had acquired, all the superiority and arrogance we had felt, would not amount to anything near the toe of one of these giants. Rather embarrassing to have this be our end. All religions that had been fighting over their different beliefs suddenly realized they had been fighting when they should have been loving. Family that hadn't spoken in years, quickly spoke. Enemies that had always hated each other, finally forgave. Everyone made one last effort to be the best version of themselves in the last few minutes before being stomped on like a bug.

All except one person.

Little Peggy Clock. A girl of six years of age, with curly red hair down to her shoulders. As far as she was concerned, she was already the best version of herself. Although, according to her gymnastics coach, her cartwheels could use a bit of work. But to Peggy, this was all rather simple. She had just learned the hard way how to deal with conflict. A few days earlier in school, she had gotten into a fight with the class bully. In actuality, it was the bully that had picked a fight with her. She learned a lot from that incident. And it was all still fresh in her head, how she would resolve conflicts from here on out.

Peggy opened her bedroom window on the second floor on that warm summer night and stuck her body out the window. She looked up to the sky, and like every other human on the planet, she saw a giant towering above. Walking about the universe like it was a field of grass, the giant was heading away from her, or at least it seemed like it. "Excuse me, giant," Peggy said out loud. She cleared her throat and then yelled louder. "Excuse me, giant!" Then suddenly, it stopped. It put its pinky into its ear as if cleaning it. Peggy took the opportunity to yell out again. "Giant!"

The giant turned and looked around itself. Its ears piqued. After thinking for a moment, or doing something for a moment, whatever that thing was, it turned around once more and bent down almost in a calculated manner, bringing its face right down to Peggy's window. A few thousand miles away of course, but it felt like it was right there due to how big its face was.

"You heard me?" Peggy asked.

"Yes. I heard you," the giant responded.

"But how? My voice is so little," Peggy asked.

"True," the giant responded. "But my ears are so big. So it works out. What is your name, little one?"

"Peggy Clock."

"My name is Clarion Ring,"

"You're a girl?" Peggy asked.

"So to speak," Clarion responded.

"Well, I'm a girl too," Peggy said. "I can show you my dresses and everything."

"That's okay. I believe you, Peggy."

"Okay. So, if I'm a girl, and you're a girl, why are you stepping on my world?" Peggy asked. Clarion's eyebrows shot up, or where her eyebrows would have been.

"Why, I don't mean to step on you, Peggy. None of us do. We're just... unaware of your existence," Clarion responded

"Well, you're aware now. Aren't you?" Peggy asked.

"Yes, we're aware. But that doesn't change much for us. You're far too small. Do you have creatures smaller than you on your planet? Much smaller, I mean."

Peggy thought for a moment to herself. "Well, I suppose, yes. Like ants," Peggy responded.

"Ants. Okay. Do your people think of them when passing by them?"

"No. My brother steps on them on purpose," Peggy added honestly.

"Okay, Peggy. Then I don't see your point, to be honest," Clarion said while scratching her bald head. She slowly raised her body, and slowly began to turn around. Clarion had a point, and Peggy knew it to be true. Why should humans be treated any better than they treat other smaller creatures? Another thing she learned in school: what goes around comes around. But there was one more thing she learned in school.

"Wait, Clarion. There is something else I want to tell you," Peggy called out. Clarion paused in her tracks once more. Her tracks, the location of which was still a mystery to humans. She turned and bent down to speak to Peggy once more.

"I'll speak to you again, Peggy. Because I took a liking to you. What would you like to say?"

"There was something I learned in school. You see, one time, Sandy tripped me while playing soccer in gym class. I was so angry. So angry!"

"I can imagine you would have been," Clarion said.

"Yes! Anyway, I was about to go trip her back," Peggy explained. "She deserved it. Anyway, just as I was about to trip her, I remembered something my teacher had taught us. She told us that when you hurt another creature, you're killing a part of yourself."

Clarion thought about that. She looked away and scratched her head.

"I'm sorry. Your teacher is not correct. I personally have hurt many creatures, and I am alive. Fully alive and well, Peggy. How do you justify this statement?"

"Don't you feel a part of you dying when you hurt someone? I killed a mosquito once and I felt horrible."

"You felt horrible, but no part of you died. And you got over it and most likely forgot what you did. It is the nature of most species to forget. And now, you're fully well," Clarion argued.

"Yes, but a part of my feelings died. The fact that I forgot is the problem. Maybe I forgot *because* a part of my feelings died."

Clarion thought about it for a second, then shook her head. "Clearly, much of what you humans teach is not correct. No part of you is dead. And as such, I'm sorry. Once again, you do not make a good point." Clarion got up, and walked away, without looking back.

Peggy called out to her. Again, and again, and again. But Clarion was off, stepping on other worlds, and kicking them through the galaxy. Clarion didn't hear Peggy anymore. And then just as Peggy was about to close her window again, and retreat into the disillusioned safety of her bedroom, she felt an earth shattering boom. She looked out her window, but couldn't see anything, not even the giants.

How could she? For the giants had been trampled on by giants one hundred times their size, and had ceased to exist.

I. Ashmawey

24

The Monster Mash

I t was atop a barren hill that the castle stood. Old, dark, decrepit. Black window shutters, crooked roof, angry gargoyles surrounding the perimeter, sitting and waiting. Cobwebs covered every corner, every nook, every angle. Each one housing an eight legged family of its own. A dead Beech tree stood at the bottom of the hill; long, skinny branches wilting down to the ground. Right beyond it, a heavy, metal gate creaked back and forth. And on that cold, dark night, the full moon rose high above the horizon, giving a bone-chilling silhouette to the old castle.

Inside the home, through the large doors that were more than twice the height of the tallest man, and past the main living room which housed a tremendous fire place, and into the great dining hall, sat a group of fascinating individuals at a long wooden table.

To one side, there was Frankenstein, face pale green, body large and solid. Next to him sat Paula the Ape Woman, with hair growing out of her face and down her head to her shoulders. Next to her was Ghost, the half visible man floating above his chair. Across from them sat Gil-man, the creature from the Black Lagoon. He was half marine and half man with gills down his scaly sides. Next to him sat Evanora, the witch with a beautiful face but a long, crooked nose and black hat to match her black dress. To her right sat Mummy, entirely wrapped from head to toe, including over his eyes. His wraps were yellowing and smelling of sand. And finally, at the head of the table, skin blank as snow, lips a crimson red, hair greased back, donning a long black cape, and two razor sharp fangs protruding out of his mouth, sat Dracula, king of the vampires.

This meeting was of the utmost importance. All of them knew it to be so, and all of them depended on it to fix what must be fixed. The first to speak, as always, was Dracula, in his Transylvanian accent that was chilling as it was twisted.

"Monsters, I thank you all for coming to my castle tonight. As you know, we have been speaking of having this meeting for some time. Years, actually." Dracula reached for his wine glass and put it up to his lips. He took a small sip of blood, closing his eyes to enjoy it for a moment before placing it back down. "We must find a solution to our problem."

I. Ashmawey

"Yes," Mummy said in a deep voice never going above a whisper. His s's were prolonged like a serpent speaking. "We must. Otherwise, it be our end."

"The new generation does not even know who I am," Gil-man said in his bubbly voice, sounding like he was underwater. "No one has even heard of me. And the older generation has entirely forgotten me."

"You think you forgottens?" Paula the Ape Woman said. Every word spoken in her deep voice came out from behind curled monkey lips which gave it all an 'oo' sound. "Not one know me! Not one!"

"Calm yourself, Paula," Dracula spoke. "Calm yourself. They do not remember us because they do not fear us."

"Fear!" Evanora the witch stood up, holding her broom. "Well, perhaps I should hex them! Let's see if they fear us then." And then she let out a long, cackling laugh.

"Hmm. Hmmhmmhmm," Frankenstein laughed with his mouth closed. He was a monster of few words.

"That won't make them fear us," Ghost said in his half-audible voice, as audible as he was visible. "That will make them hate us. Fear and hate are not the same. You will hate who you fear, but not necessarily fear who you hate."

"You're correct, my ghostly friend," Dracula commented. "They do not fear us anymore, so the question is: why not?"

"They know us," Mummy whispered," You cannot fear what you know."

"They no know me. But no fear me," Paula protested.

"You're wrong, sweetie," Evanora said. "You of all people, Mummy. Your Egyptians have known you but feared you for millennia. So why have they stopped now?!"

"Monsters," Dracula interjected. "Let us take a step back. Let us begin with a simple question, what is fear?" This was met by murmurs across the table. Frankenstein mumbled something under his breath. Ghost went from being semi-transparent to fully transparent, a useful tool to have in his arsenal. "Gil-man? Evanora? Anyone?" But no one responded.

"Fear is an emotion," Gil-man said. Dracula rolled his eyes.

"Yes, what kind of an emotion?" Dracula asked.

"An unpleasant one," Evanora added.

"Good. But one of what?" Dracula asked. Frankenstein huffed and puffed, he was sick of the questions. Then Dracula explained. "The emotion is caused by the belief that someone or something is dangerous. That something is likely to cause harm or pain. That something is a threat." The monsters thought to themselves. "There was a time when we were those things. We were scary. And we were a threat, but… other threats have since emerged. They are worse, cause more pain, and are more dangerous."

"Like what? Or who?" Ghost asked.

"Well," Dracula said. He stood up and hovered above the ground, then started circling the table. "Fear today means different things. Murderers. Rapists. Blood-loving, sadistic, gory monsters. People that feed off and enjoy the pain of others. None of us, I repeat, none of us, enjoy the pain of others."

"But Dracula, do you not literally feed on the blood of your victims?" Mummy asked.

"I do," Dracula responded. He walked away from the table, up the wall, and onto the ceiling to hang upside down. "But only to live. And I never, ever enjoy. Take my 1931 classic film, I turned my victims to vampires. And all of them, to this day, are thankful. Yes, there were some casualties, the crew of the vessel that helped us navigate to the new property, but they resisted and brought their own deaths upon themselves. Similar situation in my next film, The Return of Dracula in 1958. How many deaths in that film? How much blood did you see? 1973? 1974? What did you notice in all those films? There was no sadism." Dracula flew back down and landed atop the table, towering above the other monsters. "What about you Mummy? Your 1931 classic, how many deaths?"

"Not one," Mummy responded. "All I wanted was to reunite with my long lost love."

"Precisely. Frankenstein, yes, you had one death. And we shall not mention it due to its sadness, but it was absolutely a mistake. A mistake not in your hands, for it was how you were built. Gil-man? Evanora? Paula? And you, Ghost!? You yourself are the victim here, not the offender." The monsters nodded their heads in agreement. "Monsters, friends, today's threats are vastly beyond who we are. In entertainment, people see the grossest perversions of sadism. So much so that in our time, those who even think such things would be locked away forever so as never to come in contact with society. Now, they are lauded and applauded as storytellers and filmmakers. And outside of entertainment, people see the same lust for pain and gore on the news, in their neighborhoods, and even in their leadership." Dracula threw his hands up in question. "What shall we do?"

"Adapt," Mummy said. "Adapt or die." The monsters made some agreeing noises. Nodding their heads, hitting their broomsticks, fluttering their gills.

"Adapt?" Dracula whispered to himself. "Adapt or die? Yes, that would definitely be your choice, Mummy, wouldn't it. For immortality is your main goal." Mummy thought to himself, not knowing whether or not to take offense. "Let us talk of immortality for a moment. And as a vampire, I am equitably apt to speak of it. Why is it that we need to exist forever? Does not everyone have a temporary role on this planet?"

"Why end our existence when we have the ability not to?" Ghost asked.

"Yeah, who would want to cease existing by their own choice?!" Evanora yelled.

"Yes, yes I hear you," Dracula responded, still hovering above the table. "For me, when the world requests things of me that I cannot and will not give, especially when those things go against my very nature and what I believe to be right, then I do not wish to exist anymore."

"You no want exist anymore?" Paula asked.

"No, Paula. Not if I have to be a grotesque, soulless, monster in order to do so," Dracula responded. "My friends, we each have something that destroys our immortality. Mummy, one phrase from The Book of the Dead, Gil-man, a few more hours without water, Ghost, to enter your body once again, etc. For me, it is sunlight." He looked at the majestic, wooden grandfather clock resting against the wall. "And apropos, the sun is rising. My friends, it has been an honor to know you all. I bid thee farewell, and I hope to see you on the other side."

And with that, Dracula left the great dining hall, opened the door to his castle, and stepped outside into the sunlight.

25

The King and the Beggar

I. Ashmawey

It started when the King went for holiday. He took two personal Guards with him and traveled for a week to one of his many beach castles. Fortresses, really. Elegant and overflowing with regality, his beach properties—like all his properties—had reputations that reached every corner of the globe. No expenses spared, "Money does grow on trees, one just needs to know how to plant it," was one of his most frequented statements.

After returning from a week of lavishness, with a kingdom to rule, he comfortably seated himself nobly onto his throne. This was his domain, his sanctuary. From here, he ruled all the helpless souls who desperately needed his wisdom, guidance, and sometimes, his strong hand. Thank the Lord for the King's existence, what would the poor peasants do without him?

"Guards!" The King's smile beamed from within his puffed up chest. "The first citizen may enter." The Guards, one standing to each side of the King, hesitated as they looked to each other out of the corners of their eyes. "Have you gone deaf? Admit the first citizen! We haven't got all day." The King had a short temper.

"Your majesty," one of the Guards spoke. "There are no citizens." The King's mouth hung open. Surely, his Guards must be mistaken. His people could not survive without their noble leader, he knew that. Surely after being gone for a week, the problems of the country would have accumulated and they would be in dire desperation for their King!

"You fools, you must be looking at the wrong gate! I am sure they must have camped out for days, and therefore must be at the South gate to escape the strong winds. Go there and fetch them at once."

"Sire," the same Guard spoke again. "I did not mean there were no citizens at the castle. I meant—" he hesitated. How was he to say what he needed to say without angering the King? He had no other choice. "I meant there are no citizens in the country." To this, the King's face relayed all shades and colors before forcing a farce smile. The smile turned to a sinister chuckle and then manifested into a horrific laugh.

You may think this would make the Guards feel at ease, on the contrary.

I. Ashmawey

They trembled in their heavy boots. For they've seen the King on the worst of his days and on the best of his days, which were few and far between. The laugh became louder, it shook the royal hall and echoed off the hallowed walls. The King stood with his face towards the ceiling, hearty laughs being thrown skyward when suddenly he took out his sword and struck the Guard who spoke deep into his chest. Lifeless, the Guard hit the floor with a thump. The other Guard did not flinch, for he has been with the King long enough to know what would transpire.

"It was a fine wisecrack the Guard has joked," said the King as he wiped the blood off his sword with his red, royal cape. "But he should know better than to gag with the King. Now..." The King turned to face the remaining Guard. "Go out to the country, and find my people. And do not return until you have done so." The Guard bowed in allegiance, and began his mission. Once again, with a kingdom to rule, the King comfortably seated himself nobly onto his throne.

The King had many horrible qualities, but one of his few redeeming factors was that he could not lie to himself for too long. He knew he had sent the Guard on an impossible mission. He knew the country was empty, and he knew why. For decades, he had ruled unjustly, taxing the poor beyond their capacity, enslaving hundreds and working them to death, and worst of all, killing any and all who stood in his way. The King was more than a tyrant, and he knew that well. At times he was draconian and even sadistic. Power only creates a thirst for more, as his mother tried to explain to his father before he beheaded her.

Days passed. The King took occasional strolls through the castle. With the rooms and halls empty, a pin drop could be heard. The King didn't have a Queen. Not that he never took one. Across the years he wed five times. Of which, he hung three, one ran away, and one died of sickness... or poison. The King also didn't have a council, as he never felt he needed one. If there was one thing his father taught him when he was king, it was that anyone close to the throne would one day want it. As such, the King felt it was best to judge alone, without ever taking advice or guidance from others. He also didn't take complaint, suggestion, inquiry, not even flattery. All led to the gallows.

With days alone, the King had to prepare even his own meals. He had never in his life entered the kitchen, not even in his childhood. Day after day, the King's boredom grew. So bored, one day he even went down to the dungeons. Empty. Even the prisoners had left, meaning they had help. He recalled a time when two men came to him to judge a quarrel they had. One man had ridiculed the other for being bald. The bald man decided to wait until the first man slept, and then chopped off his hair in anger. The man with the freshly cut mane went to the King for justice. The King felt it would be just to throw both in the dungeon until which time the bald man grew hair so the first man may cut it off in vengeance. That day never came, obviously. The two spent a quarter century in the dungeons. Until this time the King went for holiday, and the entire country fled his treacherous ways.

Just as the King was about to lose his resolve, just as he was about to consider how he would change his ways if only his people would return, he heard the castle doors open. The heavy clanking of the doors echoed through the halls and into his eardrums.

He ran.

He wanted to run to the doors out of harrowing excitement but as King, he had to maintain his kingly majesty. So instead, he ran to his throne. With only seconds to spare before the Guard came into the Royal Hall, the King caught his breath. With a kingdom to rule, he comfortably seated himself nobly onto his throne. In walked the Guard. Behind him, shackled in restraints, he dragged a poor old man. His stench reached the King before anything else. How dare the Guard bring this sort of man into the castle? Still, the King was secretly thrilled to see him return to begin with.

"Guard!" The King was visibly annoyed by the repugnant smell. He turned his head away. "What is the meaning of this?" The Guard pulled the shackles strong enough that the old man was hauled forward so strongly, he landed on the hard floor in front of the King.

"Your Majesty. This is a citizen. The only one I found."

The King slowly turned enough to see the old man out of the corner of his eye.

"Bah. What a disgust," the King sneered. "What are you, exactly?"

The old man looked up, trembling. "M… m… me, sir?"

"No, the woman behind you. Of course you, you blithering fool!" The King, as always, was losing his temper.

"I am but a beggar, my Lord. Just a beggar."

"A beggar, eh? And…" The King stood up. He paced around the beggar, still on the floor with a slouched posture. How was he going to ask this question without seeming… pathetic? He'll just have to have to ask it with confidence. "Why are you here, beggar?"

"The Guard, sire. He brought me," the beggar responded. To which, the Guard landed a blow on the beggar's back making him slouch even further.

"No! Good Lord, an idiot undoubtedly. I mean, why are you still…" There was no way to ask it with confidence. "Why did you not leave with others?"

The beggar didn't know how to respond. At this point, he felt he would be destined to die no matter the cause, may as well say the truth. "To be honest my Lord, I was in a deep slumber. I was awakened by the Guard and then I learned of the citizens' departure."

"I see. A worthless creature. Wasting your life in sleep. A drunk too, undoubtedly. What is your trade, did you say?" the King asked.

I. Ashmawey

"A beggar, sire."

"Ah, right. A beggar. I see. Well, go out there and do your work."

The beggar hesitated only for a moment. He looked at the King, befuddled. He looked back at the Guard, who made no motion. Then looked to the King again. He slowly got up from the ground, and that immediately turned into a sprint for the door. For when life is at stake, even the oldest of men can run. The King watched the beggar run all the way till he vanished. He had, after all, not seen any people for days now. The King reclined back in his throne. A few more minutes and then he stood up and made his way to the gardens for some recreation, tired after a heavy day of work.

A few more days passed. The King was rested, read, eaten, relaxed, bathed, and everything else a King may do. He called to his Guard.

"Is it not time for taxes, Guard?"

It wasn't. Taxes were taken at the end of the year and that was months away. The Guard knew better, however. "It is, your majesty."

"Well then. Go fetch the taxes and return before sunset."

The Guard didn't need till sunset. He knew that. And the King knew that. But nonetheless, he agreed to obey and went out to fetch the taxes from the beggar. It was less than an hour later that he came back to the castle, and once again, threw the beggar on the floor in front of the King's feet.

Secretly pleased to see him again, the King hid his smile. "Well, well, the beggar. What have you done this time?"

The beggar tilted his head up again. "What did I do the first time, my Lord?" To this, again, the beggar received a mighty blow to his back by the Guard.

"This traitor refuses to pay tax, Your Majesty," the Guard explained.

Excited, the King stood up. "Refuses to pay taxes?!"

"My Lord, I have no money to give," the beggar swore.

"Are you not worthy of your profession?!"

"My Lord, there is no one to beg from."

"Nonsense!" the King screamed. "You are lazy, inept, and incapable of doing anything!"

The beggar smiled; to himself more than to the King. "Had my King been a capable King, I would have had people to beg."

The King's face turned to fire with anger. "Incapable, inept, lazy, and insolent!" Clenching his teeth, he spoke softly but angrily, enunciating every single syllable. "You are a traitor of the state." He looked to the Guard. "Make use of the guillotine."

The beggar laughed. He laughed and laughed and his laughter echoed through the empty halls as he was dragged away from the King. The King's face twisted with disgust. How dare he? Who did that beggar think he was? He was nothing without his King, and the people who fled were nothing too. They would surely fail to survive and beg for acceptance when they returned. Being the merciful man he was, he would accept them. But not without making an example of a few hundred of them. Just as an example, of course.

The Guard came back into the Royal Hall. A look of worry made use of his face.

"Have you relieved him of his head?" the King asked.

"Tis done, your majesty."

"Good. Bring it to me on a golden platter." The King would display his head as a trophy in his hall, a reminder that people would always require motivation to work hard. The Guard did not go, however. He shifted his feet but stood in his place. "Did I not make myself clear?"

"Your majesty..." The worrisome look on the Guard's face grew to enormous proportions. His face flushed, a bead of sweat formed on his forehead and traveled down to his cheek. "I..."

"Spit it out!"

"He escaped, Your Majesty. He left the castle."

The King's eyes surrendered into a dead openness. Wide and glaring, he examined the Guards face, peered into his soul. He shook his bones with the glare, turned his heart into a loud drum that echoed in his chest. "Why did you let him go?" the King asked. The question was so direct, so straightforward. The fact that he asked it so slightly above a whisper made it all the scarier.

"So that you may kill me, Your Majesty," the Guard responded. Suddenly, the Guards face was no longer worried. He felt comfortable, at ease.

"Why do you wish for me to kill you?"

And for the first time, the Guard smiled. "So that you may taste the fruits of your labor."

"What fruits?" the King asked. "What fruits??" The King took out his sword, took a few steps towards the Guard and stabbed him in his stomach. The Guard slowly feel to the floor. "What... fruits...?"

The Guard gasped for air as he met the last moments of his life. "Loneliness."

The King dropped his sword, letting it hit the floor making an ear deafening sound. He adjusted his cape. Alone, and with no one to rule, he comfortably seated himself nobly onto his throne.

I. Ashmawey

26

Lessons on Flying

I. Ashmawey

This instruction manual aims to prepare you for your first successful flight. Whether you have previously attempted to fly and learnt the hard way that there is more to it than simply spreading your arms and flapping them, or if you have never yet attempted to fly; out of fear, lack of confidence, or laziness, this reading is for you. Follow the steps in this manual and there will be nothing between you and being airborne. The steps outlined here are not new. They are as old as civilization. Yet, we constantly forget; we forget that we are not the first to roam the earth and we forget that those before us have already experienced what we will surely experience in our lifetimes. We forget to listen, we forget that we are not special. And because we forget, we become grounded.

1 Stop complaining that you cannot fly

Humanity has existed for hundreds of thousands of years. There are very few things that can be said in sweeping statements about all humans that ever existed... but there *are* a few. For example, no human has ever cheated death. A fact that no one can argue. Similarly, no human has ever accomplished anything by complaining. Not all things can be so simply stated, but this surely can. Many who have attempted to fly first began by complaining they cannot and will not ever be able to fly. Either their arms were too short, their bodies too heavy, their shape not aerodynamical enough, etc. If one wants to complain, they will find the opportunities endless to do so. The compelling desire to complain is no mystery. Complaining gives people a comforting feeling of kindling warmth for a finite period of time. The warmth eventually evolves into self-pity and victimization. At which time it becomes exceedingly more difficult to change the thought process. Stop complaining. The only possible outcome of complaining is more complaining.

2 Take responsibility for your failed flights

There is a clear difference between learning from past mistakes, whether yours or others', and dwelling on them. One does not succeed without failure. That does not mean however that one should live their lives lamenting over the failures of the past. Or worse, blame others for them. Every person has their thoughts on flying. Some will say flight is not possible, that we are not meant to fly in the real world, only in dreams. Others will say that flight is possible, but you are either born into a flying family or not. To be born an earth walker and then deciding to fly is not possible. Lastly, there are those who think it's possible, and people can change into it, but their methods of flying are not correct. Whatever the beliefs are that people have, they most likely were fed these thoughts by their parents who were fed them by their parents. Now comes the concern: if your inherited thoughts on flying are incorrect, and you have difficulty flying, who is to blame? Accept it as a fact, and the second rule to flying, you are responsible for your own flight. It is everyone's right to fly, given they put in the effort.

3 Decide the best flight for you

Have you ever realized just how many different kinds of flight there are? Let us first divide flight into motored and non-motored. When it comes to non-motored, there are helium, hot air, gliding, winged, just to name a few. When it comes to motored, there are equal if not more divisions. And then subdivisions, and divisions beneath that. There are divisions you never heard of, and types you could not even imagine. You will never know what the world has to offer if you do not explore. And that is what one must do first: explore. Never settle on thinking you have a flight that is best for you unless you have tried a good amount. You do not necessarily have to test-fly all types before deciding on the best, so long as you find the kind that truly makes you soar. The way to figure out if you have the right flight is simple: when you find the right kind of flight for you, you will fly internally just as much as externally. It is truly that simple.

4 Get rid of old people, and get new people

Everyone around you, every single person, will either help you fly, or deter you from it. Those closest to you, and most of the time, those who you most expect to support you, *could* actually inhibit you from succeeding. Why is that? Why is it that those around you cannot just be neutral? Why is it a fact that the people around could actually be of the type to hold you back? The answer is straightforward: because had they been the type to help you fly, they would have helped you long, long ago. They would have been themselves the type to fly. They would have been the type to urge you and teach you to fly from when you were young. It is a sad reality, but it is true. That is why you must, you absolutely must, get rid of some people. And those that you cannot get rid of, further yourself from them. For they will not support you. They will tell you what you are doing is either risky, dangerous, or impossible. They will say those who fly were born to flyers, and only those of flying blood can continue to fly. They will say you must be a flyer to learn flying, a

172

circuitous impossibility. And if you ignore them, they may sabotage your efforts. And if you persist beyond that and succeed to fly, they may come back and say that you owe them for your flight. That somehow, your flight was in part due to them and they deserve a part in your success. When this happens, remember you are not the first nor last to experience this. It is the normal cycle. Get rid of those people. And if you can, add people around you who will support you.

5 Do not waste time
Distractions are everywhere. But flying takes determination and hard work. You absolutely will not be able to fly if you waste time with distractions. This may seem like an easy thing to understand, and it is, but it is not an easy thing to remember. You must constantly remind yourself, as distractions are so plentiful and they are in many cases tempting. Of course, there will always be those who prefer to pretend to fly instead of actual flight. But what kind of person would rather sit behind a lit up screen pretending to fly when they can actually be soaring through the clouds? Who would prefer to sit for days, months, and years watching other people fly and follow the intricacies of their lives flying when they themselves should be flying instead? If only they used their time more efficiently, they would not be observing anymore, they would be doing.

6 Soar, and never stop
When you start soaring, for the love of all that is holy, never stop. Fly high above the earth, looking down through the clouds at those who wasted their lives walking on dirt. Look up at the stars and planets above you. Look ahead at your kindred birds and creatures of the sky. Never stop flying. Never touch the ground again.

I. Ashmawey

27

Of Honor and Grace

Of honor.

I put quill to parchment, not knowing what the good Lord shall allow to come to me. What shall come through the wisdom of my soul to this writing? Whatever comes, it shall be my truest, unfiltered thoughts.

It started a fortnight ago when my husband died. King Jamison the First, a noble, strong, and just leader of our country. The fairest in many decades. Unlike any of his predecessors, he visited with the villagers frequently and many of the times, without guards. He would learn of their difficulties and issues, help them in the best way he can, and then travel back up to the castle in the evening. It was not until two weeks ago that an angry villager from another country came into ours and attacked the noble King. He approached him near the fjord before the eastern border and brutally and savagely killed him.

According to our country bylaws, I was to assume power for precisely one week, just enough time to crown our son who is ten years of age. The first thing I did was address our people. I asked for it to be officially written that I asked for our people to support their temporary queen in this time of hardship. That they will be safe, and that the country will be safe. That we will continue to prosper and live in justice and harmony. And that, lastly, I will find the King's murderer and bring him to justice.

That was the second thing I did. I hunted the murderer down till he was brought down on his knees in my the royal hall. Against the wishes of my advisors, I decided to first speak to the murderer personally.

"My question for you is simple, why did you do what you did?" I asked him.

"Your husband was a thief," the man said.

"And so you decided to kill him? Without first accusing him of this yourself?" I asked. The man shuddered. He did not have an answer. "You will be returned to your country where you will be tried and judged by your own King for your crimes." Some saw it as weakness. Others saw it as merciful. But all agreed that it was just.

My next order of duty, still before getting a chance to grieve, was to crown my ten-year-old son.

I. Ashmawey

My ten-year-old son.

He had no desire to lead a country or even be crowned. Days it took me to convince him to accept. The understanding we had was simple, I would govern, and he would appear regal. That much, he did agree to.

And so I governed. I met with the Lords. I made decisions regarding our economy and our agriculture. I ruled between many who had conflict with one another. I aided the poor. I provided sustenance for the sick.

Of grace.

As I write this now, a memory comes to mind. It is a faint memory, one that I had not recalled in many, many years. And I have not an understanding of why I recalled it today. I was young, no more than five years of age. My father, a nobleman in the country at the time, was drunk. It was late into the hours of the night. I woke from bed and crawled out onto the cold floor. I found my father sitting next to the fire, drinking more. He looked at me and smiled. He took down another gulp of ale before speaking.

"You almost did not survive, my dear," he said. I did not respond, just looked at him. "You had two sisters before you. I killed them both, you see. I buried them alive. For our traditions teach that if you sacrifice your females, the Lord will then gift you with males. So I did. I buried them. The second one, I waited till she was your age. Why? I do not know. Perhaps to further my cruelty." I continued standing there. I understood, I comprehended. But I did not respond. I couldn't. "The second one, why, she helped me dig her own grave. Not knowing what it was for. She would..." he paused. He sniffled and quickly wiped a tear from his eyes. "She would wipe the dirt off my hair as I dug." He looked me right in the eyes before continuing to speak. "And then I killed her. But with you, I couldn't. I couldn't do it for the third time. I couldn't do it!" he screamed at me. He fell to his knees in a fit of tears and grabbed me bringing me closer to his chest.

I hugged him back. "It's alright, father," I said to him. And we never spoke of that incident, nor the incidents mentioned therein, again. And like my sisters whom I have never met were buried beneath the dirt, I too buried their memories, and the memory of that night, in the deepest depths of my mind and soul.

And so it is on this day that I ask a question, one that my mind has never come across before. Not out of fear or worry, but simply because the possibility of this question's existence never was an option. The question, in all simplicity: what if I was lied to? In that moment with my father, many years ago, I did not question his actions. Nor did I feel they were wrong. I believed for all intents and purposes that I was an inferior being, not favored by God. God created many creatures to walk upon the earth. There was man, and then there was all others: women, dogs to be companion, horses upon to ride, cows whose milk to drink, and so on. But unlike dogs, horses, and cows, I speak. I think. I reason. And in this moment, I write.

It is true that the holy Church has proclaimed that I, as a woman, do not have a soul. But what if they are wrong? I speak to the Lord, same as any man. I feel His presence. I have governed this country, the same as my husband. But of course, behind the guise of a young man who is my son. I have acted justly, and fairly. And I have treated the people well.

The question I ask is not whether or not I, as a woman, am equal to man. The question I ask is: what if I was lied to? What if, to live my life to the fullest, I must unlearn everything I have ever learned and begin from scratch, accepting only what is fact to be truth?

I am now imprisoned, for my writings have been found by the council. My ten-year-old son has proclaimed me a heretic. He has sentenced me to death by hanging. Tomorrow morning, my life is to be taken away from me. The life that the good Lord has given me, is to be taken away by somebody else. Because I have dared ask a question. Asking a question means that I am not submissive. Not being submissive means that I may cause problems, as others may follow my lead. And that may mean things could change, in a world where people want everything to remain the same. I hope whoever reads this will do one thing: ask questions, even if takes you to the gallows.

I. Ashmawey

28

October Words

I. Ashmawey

Mild sunlight on cool, still air. Dead leaves cracking under fickle, excited feet. Orange, red, yellow everywhere. A spicy aroma flying through windows of living homes, draped in death. Farce spiders standing on linen webs, covering patios housing dread. One orange vegetable claims fame for the month, filling every porch. Candy in plenty, eyes wide open, pails empty, skeletons dancing, witches brewing, mummies wrapping, werewolves howling, alas... it's Halloween.

I looked at the costume laying on my bed. Captain Hook, complete with sword, hat, wig, coat, and of course, the hook. I felt the excitement running through my veins like a fire taking over my body.

Captain Hook wasn't my first choice. Initially, I wanted to be a vampire. This was my first Halloween, and the classical attribute of Dracula demanded I don that outfit. I then wanted to be Spock. For a while, I had convinced my family to each take a Star Trek character. That didn't last long though, eventually they decided on pirates. And since matching my family was important, a pirate I would be.

It felt strange putting on the costume. Being my first, I didn't know what to expect. The plastic feel of the clothes was a new sensation against my inexperienced skin. The different pieces of the costume looked to be different material: cotton, velvet, linen, but they all felt like plastic. I slipped my arms through the coat. Majestic. How could anyone see me and not want me to command a pirate ship? The wig, I didn't enjoy so much. The feeling of the fake hair falling across my face and cheeks was not an enjoyable experience. To be honest, it irritated me far too much. But it was absolutely worth it. The hat was regal, it gave me a majestic feeling I forever yearned for. And the sword, it gave me an amazing strength.

What really made all the difference though, what made me truly feel like the iconic Captain Hook, was, of course, the hook. The moment I grasped the cheap hollow plastic, I completely transformed into the immortal legend. Fully convinced, fully embodied. I was ready in that moment to face any fear and any foe. But what I really wanted was to see my friends. To show them who I was becoming for the night.

It was a sad affair that not all my friends enjoyed this night, this week, this month-long occasion. A twelfth of the year spent being fully engulfed, a time of true escapism to taste a side of ourselves we usually bury deep. It wasn't about the death, the blood, the gore. It wasn't about the graveyards, the skeletons, the severed limbs dripping red sugar water. It was about embracing our fears, whatever they may be. To be, accept, and enjoy being scared. It was about the thrill of welcoming this emotion with arms wide open and seeing where it can take us. That's what Halloween was.

But not all people saw it like that. I had friends who had been taught by their parents this holiday was about worshipping the devil. They were taught it was a Pagan superstition from before people became Godly and learned the correct religion. They were taught that to celebrate Halloween was to forsake all that is holy, and anger God by disobeying His commandments. I don't claim to speak for God, I don't understand how anyone can. But I do believe that those who say such things probably don't understand what it is that God wants very much.

I hopped down the stairs, one step at a time. For with every step, the air dense with the smell of pumpkin pie surrounded me more. My strides became faster until I jumped off the last few steps, making my way into the kitchen. I was going to sneak a few bites of the pie sitting to cool. For nothing, absolutely nothing, tasted better than fresh pumpkin pie.

The clock struck six. And on cue, all the wonderfully horrific lights came on. Dangling across the walls, orange stars lit up the house. On the front patio, every jack-o-lantern came to life. Exhibiting happy yet creepy smiles, exemplifying what was best about this holiday: the mixture of joy and fear. Or better yet, being joyful *because* you're being fearful. To those who knew what it meant, they felt it perfectly. For those who did not, they would never feel it anyway. I walked across the patio, examining all the lanterns, ensuring they were all on. Motion sensors set off sounds of laughing ghosts. I watched as the inflatable Mickey and Minnie came to life, growing in size to their utmost ability. Mickey with his vampire costume, Minnie with her witch hat, both standing over another beautifully happy and scary jack-o-lantern. I ran my fingers over the front bushes, feeling the fake cobwebs. Small spiders, randomly scattered throughout. I had one pumpkin that I carved myself, it didn't look nearly as symmetrical as the plastic ones. But yet, mine was perfect.

Back inside, I poured bags of candy into a witch's brewing pot. It seemed almost an impossibility for me not to sneak a few into my mouth. I suppose Halloween was all about sneaking, wasn't it?

I sat down on the couch, a few minutes of calmness before the night began. Excited as I was, I reminded myself that I wasn't young anymore. Thirty years old, and about to experience my first Halloween. My son and daughter came down the stairs, both in their pirate's apparel. As much as I wanted my first Halloween to be a vampire one as I said, seeing those two younglings running down happily, ready to scream "Ahoy, mateys!" was a priceless affair. I smiled at them, watching their innocent, happy faces excited for the night ahead of them. Following behind them was my wife dressed as Tinkerbell, the perfect companion to pirates.

"Arggg!" I screamed at them, holding up my hook.

"Ahoy!" they screamed, and so we clanked our swords together. For this was the most fun they would have in a long time. I looked at them, and I was thankful that though I grew up believing something in particular about this celebration — about many celebrations—I was able to think outside my own box and re-examine things on my own. Unlike my friends who grew up with my same beliefs, I was able to think for myself.

I understood perfectly that this night was about my kids. As Halloween is always about the kids. But in that moment, I could not lie to myself. For I too, was a kid at heart. This was, after all, my first Halloween. And while I wanted my children to enjoy every second, I too was going to enjoy. This was going to be my special night, thirty years in the making. All the missed school Halloween parties when I wanted to dress up, all the lost candy I would have attained after the uttering of three innocent words, all the different characters I fell in love with and wanted to pretend to be one year after the other, everything I had ever missed was going to be enjoyed on that night.

And what a night it was.

I. Ashmawey

29

The Annual Exam

I. Ashmawey

My name is Mariel. I love my name, and perhaps I wouldn't have had this name if it wasn't for the new law. Although I was against it at first, over the years it has proven to be one of the best changes our government has ever put in place: the annual exam. One, simple, exam at the beginning of each year. The exam is an oral one, and it drastically changes from year to year, and even from person to person. It usually consists of ten questions, all asked by a professional known as an Examiner. Some of the questions were case studies, some were behavioral, and one or two were technical.

One question I was asked a few years back was: if you are on the surface of Earth, and you walk one mile south, one mile west, and one mile north, where will you end up? Or: if you could send a message to the entire world, what would you say in thirty seconds?

Each exam gets graded on a level of 1 to 100. And if you receive 70 or above, you are permitted to speak in public for the duration of that year. Otherwise, you were temporarily banned from any form of it. Public speaking included but was not limited to social media, blogging, articles, publications, radio, television, even standing in a town square and speaking to a crowd of more than five people. The permissible number of people became ten people if they were your family and it was a pre-registered family function such as a birthday or public holiday.

Before you begin judging this law and this system as most everybody did at first, including yours truly, I ask you to spend a few minutes recalling times from your life when you heard someone say something and you thought to yourself, in all bluntness, *That is the dumbest thing I have ever heard.*

I mentioned my name earlier, Mariel. I'm lucky, I happen to absolutely love my name. But yes, I have experienced many times when I saw a child and thought to myself, *How dare the parent name the child that name? How is there not a law against this? The parent is absolutely vile and cruel for doing so. After all, the child will be the one to suffer. How is this not regulated?*

Nevertheless, that is a small example.

How about convincing almost a thousand people to take their own lives such as in Jonestown in 1978? Convincing people to eat or not eat in a certain way or to take or not take certain medication? How about starting wars? How about on a much smaller scale, backbiting or eliciting a conflict between two innocent people? How about slander?

I can easily go through the centuries and millennia of civilization and count off the examples of when people spoke who should not have spoken. But I do not think this is necessary. I think you have a solid understanding now as to why this was deemed a good idea by almost everyone. Especially in the internet age.

We have been living in peace, prosperity, and happiness. And those who have broken the law have been imprisoned. And in actuality, the number of those imprisoned have been less and less lately. And so you know, I am a young woman of sound mind and age. I am logical, learned, and progressive. And I wholeheartedly believe this is the correct way of life.

A knock came at my door.

"Can I help you?" I asked opening my door. A middle aged man with a black top hat stood with a briefcase under his armpit.

"Mariel Carol?" he asked. I nodded. "A pleasure. May I come in please?" I nodded once again. He was wearing a full black suit and black leather shoes. He came straight into the living room and sat on the comfortable brown leather reclining chair. I was still standing but found it awkward to do so. So I sat on the couch next to him. He opened the briefcase and pulled out a binder with hundreds of pieces of paper. He began flipping through the pages, pausing intermittently to reread something, then continued flipping.

"I'm sorry, who are you?" I asked.

"I am an Examiner."

"Examiner? But, I had my exam in January. As always," I responded.

"Indeed you did Madame. However, this is a re-examination."

"A re-ex— There's no such thing!" I screamed.

"Of course there is. The law was set forth last year that if the government finds it necessary, any citizen shall be re-examined at any time."

Finds it necessary?

"And why does the government find it necessary for me?" I asked.

He continued flipping through the pages. "That's precisely what… I am… Ah! Here we are." He cleared his breath. "On the fifteenth of April, at seven thirty-two in the evening, at the Tam O'Shanter Restaurant on Los Feliz Blvd in the city of Los Angeles, county of Los Angeles, State of—"

"I know where it is! What about it?" I asked impatiently.

"You said, and I quote, 'Of course the President wants to do that. It directly benefited his company.' End quote."

My mouth hung open. Was he serious? "What in the hell is your point?"

"Mariel Carol, by publically—"

"It wasn't public! It was with one friend over prime rib and a cheese plate," I said.

"It was in a public setting. And by publicly questioning the President's political actions, you were enticing public unrest, skewing public opinion, and stirring up the public into anarchy."

"I… was eating… prime rib," I said. Slowly, and thoughtfully. The Examiner looked at me quietly.

"Mariel Carol," he started.

"Just Mariel."

"Four individuals sitting at a table near your heard your words. One of them went home, began researching the President and his company. He then began researching if there was, in fact, a connection between his political actions and his personal gain. He then continued to write an article for a very reputable online magazine which he works for, entirely about this matter. The article was published this morning, people are talking about it, and I am here talking to you. So, Mariel Carol—"

"Just Mariel."

"I have been asked to re-examine you. And you must cooperate."

"You know what?" I said. "Fine. Go ahead."

"Are you ready right now?" he asked.

"Yes. I've always been a proponent of the annual exam. While I disagree with the notion of being re-examined and I disagree that I, of all people, need to be re-examined, especially for what I said, fine. By all means. Go ahead."

"Very well," he said as he flipped through a few more pages. "Mariel Carol. Your first question is as follows: how do you feel about the President's latest political actions that took place on the morning of April fifteenth of this year?"

Oh my God.

"Are you serious?" I asked. "That's the first question?"

"Is that your answer, Mariel Carol?" he asked.

"I'm not answering that question! This is outrageous!" I screamed. "I see exactly what it is you're doing here! Don't think I don't see it!" The Examiner closed his binder, put it back in his briefcase, and put the briefcase under his armpit.

"Where are you going?" I asked.

"The re-examination is finished. Mariel Carol, you have been sentenced to Not Speaking for the remainder of this calendar year. You will be examined again at your regular date at the beginning of next year."

"What! No!" I screamed. "No! Please!" I tried to grab him as he opened my front door.

"Must I remind you, Mariel Carol, the door is now open. Anything you say will be public." I immediately shut my mouth. "Have a good day." He walked out of the house.

And I closed the door behind him. Behind him, and in front of me.

30

Friendship Atop a Mountain

Angel's Landing was a sight for the angels. It was one of the de facto classic hikes in Zion National Park and one of the most stunning viewpoints one could ever experience. But it's not recommended for anybody with a fear of heights. Starting at the Grotto Trailhead, the hike to Angels Landing followed the longer West Rim Trail up and out of the west side of the main canyon. It was a unique fin-like mountain formation that juts out to the center of the main canyon.

This hike usually takes between two and six hours; your legs will burn, your knees may shake, and the view will take your breath away!

On one particular day, I hiked alone. It was a conscious decision I had made. Though I had never vacationed alone before, and wasn't usually accustomed to being without constant company, for this experience, I felt I needed the silence of solitude. A gift few in the modern world were blessed with.

From the beginning of the entire hike, I was not conscious of anything around me. I have the strange ability to completely zone things out sometimes. I used to think it was only when I was physically active that my mind was able to go into this mental astral projection. But I've succeeded in doing so even while sitting in a movie theater watching a film that I was completely unengaged in.

So while hiking, my body moved but my mind was elsewhere. I simply followed the signs and kept on going up, up, up.

After roughly four hours of consistent, nonstop movement, I got to the top of the hike. And for the first time since I began my trek, I straightened my back and looked up to the sky. An exquisite Peregrine Falcon flew across the clouds above me. No matter how high I went, the birds would always be higher.

I allowed the sight in front of me, around me, to completely take me over. Before me, a deep canyon carpeted with greens spread wide. In the middle of it, a crystal blue creek ran like a ribbon to the end of nowhere. On both sides, solid red rocky mountains slept like hardened clay. Etched into them, the definitive wrinkles of age. Behind them, a wallpaper of blue and white reaching across the horizon. To say it was a heavenly sight would be the harshest of understatements.

"This," I said out loud to myself, "is a sight that rejuvenates the soul." I turned my head to the left and then slowly all the way to the right. Taking in every inch of the view in front of me. "If only people could see this."

"They could," a voice said from behind me. I spun my entire body around. Who was that? Not a soul in sight. The voice, it couldn't have been imagined. It was so incredibly deep and barely sounded human. Almost as if a lion were speaking.

"Who said that?"

"I cannot tell you. You must learn who I am," the voice said again. I couldn't get over how deep it was. Someone must have been playing a trick and using some kind of voice modifier.

"Is this a trick?" I asked.

"There is no deception," the voice said. I continued to look around me, turning my body three hundred and sixty degrees a number of times. I looked up, I looked down, nothing.

"Who is this?!" I screamed. My heart began beating faster.

"You know who I am," the voice said. "You praised me only a moment ago." I felt the voice in my chest, trembling through my body. Just as I was about to retreat, to climb down the entire hike that I had labored to come up, I took a moment to think to myself. If I felt this voice inside my body, and it was too deep to be coming from a human, what could it possibly be?

"Are you…" I hesitated. "Are you the mountain?"

"I am."

"How is this happening?" I whispered to myself. "I'm speaking to the mountain? How is that even possible?"

"It is possible because you are worthy," the voice said. I didn't know where to look, for I was standing on the mountain itself. I had no idea how to have this conversation, so I sat down, and then I laid on my back. Peering up to the heavens, I took a deep breath. I fixated my eyes on the sky above, past the moving clouds.

"Have you spoken to others?" I asked.

"Yes. So many I have spoken to over the ages. But not in many, many years," the mountain responded.

"Why has it been so long? Were others…" and I felt arrogant even asking, "not worthy?"

"Precisely. I speak to any who want to listen. Wanting to listen is, in fact, enough to make one worthy."

"That's impossible. Anybody, everybody would want to listen," I said.

"If only that were true, my friend. Thousands come here each year and stand on me. But not one of them speaks to me."

"Well you can't expect them to speak to you when they don't know you can speak," I explained. "After all, I didn't exactly speak to you."

"You did not. But you did notice me. You acknowledged me, and my existence," the mountain said. "You talked of your soul, and how it may be rejuvenated."

"And I meant it," I affirmed. "It's not just the sights and the views, it's the feeling. The vitalization I got." There was a silence, as I felt the mountain connect with me. "How long have you existed?"

"I do not know. Many epochs, many periods. It is difficult to know exactly how long. I was here when the dinosaurs walked the earth. They lived peacefully. Never shedding blood except for sustenance. They never sought too much, nor too little. Many creatures came after, all living in a similar way. They embraced me and nature, and I embraced them. But this was many, many years ago, my new friend."

"How have we been since then? Humans, I mean," I asked.

"Man," it began, "you are a young species, still finding your way. I recall encountering those who wore feathers. They too did not desire much. And they felt it prudent to preserve me. And in those days, I naively thought all man would not differ much from other creatures. Until of course, man began changing."

"How did we change?" I asked.

"At one time, you knew what you wanted. Now, you live life heedlessly. No point, no goal, no purpose. Even when you seek more and more greedily, you do not even know what it is you truly seek. Or how much of it. Or what you will do with it. You simply want more." I didn't immediately respond to that. I myself did not know what I wanted. "You may notice, my new friend, that even the creatures before man at least knew what they wanted. What does that say about those creatures?" it asked.

"What does it say about us?" I asked in return.

"You ask the right questions, my friend. You will do well in your given time here on this planet," the mountain said.

I sat up. I touched my hand to the mountain beneath. "What about you? What is your purpose in your time here?" I asked.

"To inspire people like you," the mountain responded. "The few who come and see me, not to boast it, but to seek inspiration."

"Thank you," I said.

I. Ashmawey

31

The Young Man and the Sea

They told me never to miss a sunset.

Play the games, eat at the buffets more than the restaurants, watch the shows once and twice, enjoy the pool and the gym, I heard it all and I heard it from all sorts of people. But the one thing everyone agreed on was that under no circumstances should I ever miss a sunset on a cruise. But I had missed them all, and I waited for my last night on the cruise before I decided to see one.

My wife and I had finally been able to put the kids to bed early that night, a full day at the pool had worn them out. Looking at my wife, she seemed more exhausted than they were.

"You feeling okay, love?" I asked.

"Yeah, honey. I'm just beat. Aren't you?" she asked.

"Physically, yes. But my mind is racing for some reason. I'm going to take a walk on the deck for some air. Don't stay up." And with that, I kissed her goodnight and left the room. She was perfectly aware of my recent struggles. Lately, I had been spending much of my time in contemplation, trying to find my place in this world.

Sure, I had a good paying job, and I was decently successful in it. But I knew I could do more, that I was destined for more. I knew I could make an impact on the world before I departed it, but I hadn't a clue how. And nothing I tried succeeded. My friends didn't share my same agonies, they were perfectly content living day by day, enjoying the smaller things in life with no real goals, ambitions, or plans.

I stepped out into the most open space I had ever been in. I stood in the sky. Surrounded by sleepy clouds and a departing sun. I looked out at the glaring yellow as it shattered my eyes, desperate to use all its strength to proclaim its power. But time, stronger than all earthly beings, pulled it down faster than my vision could notice.

"Goodbye, old friend," I said softly to the sun. "When I see you next, I hope to be a changed man." A pod of dolphins ritualistically jumped in the distance, bidding the sun farewell and welcoming the silence of the night. I had a strange thought in the moment, I wished the dolphins were sharks. And then I wished the sharks would attack the ship and jump up at me—but from a safe distance. What would I do in such a situation?

Then I realized what I would do; I would immediately pull out my phone, take a video of the encounter, and post it somewhere. To be known as one of the few that had an unfiltered encounter with a shark. How lame of me. Instead of seeking a true, real-life adventure, I just imagined a false one from a safe distance. And I didn't even imagine an actual one, just something to post online about.

I looked up at the sky I was standing in as I rested my elbows on the port side handrail of the ship. I was quickly put in a trance watching the canvas above become a decorated tapestry. It began with large strokes of lavender paint slowly becoming darker. And like an accidental tipping of a glitter bottle, minute twinkles began appearing across my sight. And what a sight it was, knowing they've been there all along but only now being able to witness them as they opened their eyes. The lavender began disappearing, for it too had had its time. And slowly the black awakened from a deep slumber, taking over the night.

The waves below crashed rhythmically against the side of the massive floating city. There was a very slight rocking, one you could only feel if you closed your eyes and waited for it. I looked out onto what was now a dark inhabitation, a black piece of fabric covering my sight with tiny pinholes that dared not shine too bright. The line between the sky and the water was gone. They became one, happy, and content together.

So this was it?

People spoke of the ocean, and how peering out onto the water changed their lives. They also spoke of the stars, and how looking up at them gave them wisdom. I was looking out onto both, but to be honest, I didn't feel anything changing. In movies, books, songs, and even stories I heard from elders, many people have had reflective nights that were turning points in their lives. That one night when they thought to themselves alone, reassessing their entire beings and existences, and coming to massive conclusions where they became different people.

I looked down to the water, it didn't change me. Seeing the waves come back and forth up to the ship did nothing for me. It was so ritual, so repetitive, the same thing kept happening over and over and over.

Something coming from inside me told me to keep looking. It told me that maybe, just maybe, a wave will come differently. That it will come higher, lower, stronger, softer. That it will come and not go, or one will go and not come back again. But none of that happened. Though with every new wave, I had a small hope it would be different. But just as soon as it would arrive, I would realize it was like the others. And then it would retreat without leaving a dent on the gigantic vessel I inhabited.

I didn't understand why so many had spoken about learning from the ocean. I had even heard that those who lived by the water were different, that it altered their personalities. But, being honest with myself, I had gained nothing.

I walked down the deck, taking small simple steps. Once I set my feet in motion, I let my mind return back to the heavens and allowed my body to take care of the easy work.

As I walked, I continued looking up at the sky. There they were, the ancient stars. The twinkles and sparkles that were as old as time. Dictating rulers came and went, empires rose and fell, new civilizations plowed through the old, but the stars still sat. Watching, observing, in a sense, protecting. But most of all, waiting for us to get our act together. They were so far away, so wise. Part of a large dosser hanging from the heavens that cannot be changed or altered by us no matter what we did.

Sure, they were beautiful. It was sometimes difficult to remember that they weren't just decorations hanging from a ceiling but that they were actual entities billions of miles away. The sky above us is in fact nothingness for what may as well be an eternity.

If anything, it made me feel so small, smaller than I've ever felt before. But, actually, my whole world was small. Everything was so tiny, an infinitesimal speck in the saga of history. And everybody, every single person from the first man till the last woman will look up at these same stars that protect us and think about their lives. People always spoke about looking up to them and hearing much of what their souls hid. I didn't feel that way.

What did I feel then? What was I doing? Why was none of this working? Here I was, taking time to think alone. My strenuous childhood and working hard in school and killing myself with studying in college and slaving at my job and paying taxes and taking care of my family and trying to find my purpose ANDTHENWHAT!? And here I was, on vacation to clear my mind. Taking a walk in the middle of the night to even further clear my mind… and nothing. I've come to no conclusions and I've received no revelations. Maybe it was all fake, all the stuff I'd been hearing about meditation and time alone and sunsets.

I went back to the rail and rested my elbows on it.

Speak to me.

For the love of God, speak to me.

And then there was light. From behind the darkness, from the furthest of furthers, there was light. Breathing life into the dead sky, bringing colors into the plainness, the light came. And with every inch it traveled, it uncovered the secrets of the night. Then the sun awoke from its deep sleep. And without being able to help it, without ever realizing it, I smiled.

"Good morning, old friend," I said softly to the sun. "I think…" and then I thought. I thought about everything that crossed my mind that night. I thought about my place in the world.

I will continue to look for it, I will never stop.

I. Ashmawey

But perhaps… perhaps the journey is the destination after all. "I think I am a changed man."

The sunrise was beautiful, giving me a new day, new hopes, new dreams. A sight that would change my life.

32

Panspermia

"I'm not a religious scholar, gentlemen," I said. I had a hint of zeal in my tone, but more so, confidence. "I am a scientist. So it would be foolishly ignorant of me to speak to you of how your individual respective faiths should or should not relate here."

"Miss Hepburn," the Priest spoke, "we understand and appreciate your diplomatic courtesy. All we ask is you that understand ours."

"I do," I responded.

"All we are saying is that a discovery of this magnitude needs years to study, and even longer to confirm," the Imam seated next to the Priest explained. "Nothing should be publicized until it has been fully vetted by all stakeholders."

"Moreover," the Rabbi, and third of the bunch, chimed in, "you announcing it now is sure to stir much of public opinion, and therefore cause general unrest. You must recognize that." He took a deep breath, calming his nerves. "You must."

I sat there, looking at the screen in front of me where three aged men sat piercing me with their eyes. They sat together, bound as brethren for the first time. Staring at me, the common threat that glues their kinship.

The question was a simple one, though oftentimes the simplest are the most difficult. The question: was there life on Jupiter? You see, life on Earth is composed primarily of hydrogen, oxygen, carbon, and nitrogen. If we thoroughly tested Jupiter for these four elements, and we tested the ratios and proportions existing of each and compared to Earth's, then perhaps we would be able to arrive at a number, a probability that life ever existed on Jupiter.

I was still one day away from arriving back on earth. And I knew, deep down in the depths of their hearts, that they would rather I not return.

Oh, none of that now. Who am I to speak for their desires?

"Miss Hepburn," the Priest began again.

"Commander Hepburn," I responded.

"Very well, Commander. Do you consider yourself a scientist or an astronaut?" he asked. I didn't understand. I understood the question but did not at all understand the relevance of it.

I. Ashmawey

"I am Commanding Science Pilot of the U.S.S. Responsum. So, by nature of my profession, I am both," I responded.

"So you feel like you are a woman of science, and a woman of exploration?" he continued.

"Yes."

"The Responsum…" the Imam began. "May I ask, that naming, what's its significance?"

"I believe you know, sir. I believe you all do," I responded. They knew, but they were trying to manipulate the conversation. "The Responsum is Latin for The Answer. And that's the purpose of the Responsum. Its sole directive is to attain a solid answer for the question."

"One last question, Miss Hepburn," the Rabbi spoke softly.

"Commander."

"Are you a woman of faith?" the Rabbi asked.

"I am," I responded immediately.

"Which?" the Rabbi inquired further.

"Irrelevant," I responded. "But I will say this. And it's the last thing I will say. Mankind interpreted faith and religion many years ago, and we developed a system of faith that reconciles with life. And as we learned more about our world, some of us turned a blind eye to the discoveries. Others decided to use these discoveries to reinterpret faith so that our understanding of it is more accurate. The discovery of dinosaurs is an example." I took a pause.

I was going to do it, there was no way around that fact. But every word I said would either make my life easier or more difficult. "Gentlemen, we are at the doorway to yet another discovery. Listen to me closely please, this discovery does not challenge or threaten your faiths. Rather, it only challenges you to spend the time and effort to reinterpret your own, personal, human, possibly fallible, understanding of your faiths."

There was a long pause. The three looked to each other, communicating hundreds of words through their eyes before looking back to the screen at me.

"Miss Hepburn," the Imam began.

"Yes?" I said.

"Do you plan on continuing with your announcement?" he asked.

Unbelievable.

It's like he didn't hear a single word I had said. They had their concerns, and they had their motivations, and they cared about nothing else.

"Yes. The press conference will take place moments after I arrive," I responded. I tried not to speak with any arrogance in my heart. I was, after all, the possessor of power in this situation. I had in my hands a simple statement my lips would utter that could… *could*… destroy the entire purpose of their existences.

Only if they let it.

"Very well, Miss Hepburn," the Priest said somberly. Like he had truly believed they would have been able to change my mind. "You made a premature discovery. You understand the implications of unleashing it upon the world when mankind is not yet ready. You have been warned of the catastrophic possibilities that may unfold. And you have decided to continue upon this path. Very well. We wish you the best."

"Sir, with due respect to you all, you are mistaken," I answered. "You say that mankind isn't ready. Am I not mankind? The fact that we have made this discovery is proof enough that we are ready. If we weren't, we wouldn't have found... wait a minute. What do you mean a premature discovery?"

The three men snickered to each other. A simple bomb planted in the conversation, ticking for a few seconds. "That's correct," the Rabbi responded. "It would not be the first and certainly not the last time science announces something, a breakthrough so to speak, that is very far from being verified. A discovery, my child, is not enough to go off of."

I smiled at the men. We said our goodbyes and cut communication. He was correct. A discovery was not enough to go off of. But it wasn't simply a discovery. We had hardcore evidence.

I turned the screen back on and brought up the speech I had written. I was going to go through it one more time. Not that I was going to make any changes to appease the men, but... but what? I had already reviewed it endlessly. Every last syllable had become second nature to me. Then why was I reviewing it again? I should be honest, shouldn't I? At least with myself. Nevertheless, the file was opened.

"Ladies and gentlemen," I read to myself out loud. "Fellow Americans, fellow men, women, and children, fellow humans, my name is Lynn Hepburn. I am the Commanding Science Pilot of the U.S.S. Responsum." Then I began typing a sentence that was not there before, and I read it out loud as I typed. "Our mission, as our ship's name implies, is to attain a response, an answer. To what question? Simply: is there life on Jupiter?" I typed the question mark, then went back to reading. "We have come to the conclusive outcome that there is no life on Jupiter." I exhaled a sigh. "Nonetheless, we have made a fantastic discovery. While life on Jupiter does not exist, there was a time when it did. We have conclusive evidence that roughly four billion years ago, there was in fact life on Jupiter. While the details of that life are still unknown, we know one thing for sure: life on Earth began with life on Jupiter."

I paused there. Was I really going to say this? While I had been so incredibly sure, and so incredibly excited, and so incredibly... alive... to say this to the world, now I seem hesitant. I was so sure, so what happened? Had I really allowed those men to make me doubt whether or not I should make this announcement. It's true, it's fact, it's real, so then why hesitate? "In a process called panspermia, we have evidence to show that an asteroid that hit Jupiter four billion years ago lifted certain microbial entities from the planet's surface and traveled to Earth, landing somewhere around the present day Mediterranean Sea. From there, life on Earth began. From there, you and I were born. And from there, a few of us went and visited our first home. And now we return with answers."

There was more. Much more. But I had read what I wanted to read. I was going to do this, and nothing was going to stop me. I was now sure of myself, more than ever.

The next day, after the landing process had concluded, the entire team of the U.S.S. Responsum was back home. The press conference was to take place right outside the shuttle doors as soon as the team exited. I was ready, pressed and dressed. There were no butterflies in my stomach, only happiness and elation. I stood at the shuttle doors waiting to breathe unprocessed oxygen for the first time in years.

As soon as the door began opening, I forgot about my mission, I was just excited to be home. To see the sun shining bright enough to feel the warmth on my skin. Birds. I wanted to hear real birds, rather than the sound files I had been hearing through my headphones. My mom, my dad, my little sister. I couldn't wait to see them all.

The heavy door had finished opening and my team and I were greeted with a beautiful sky. I climbed up the ladder, every step giving me more pure air—

News Report:

On the fourteenth of June, Lynn Hepburn, Commanding Science Pilot of the U.S.S. Responsum, was murdered. She had just returned from a two year trip to Jupiter for scientific research. Upon exiting the aircraft, the moment her head had been in view, Hepburn was hit with a bullet between her eyes. The killer is unknown. While some of Hepburn's science reports are clear enough for her team to understand, much of the truth of her discoveries will be buried with her.

33

My Two Dreams

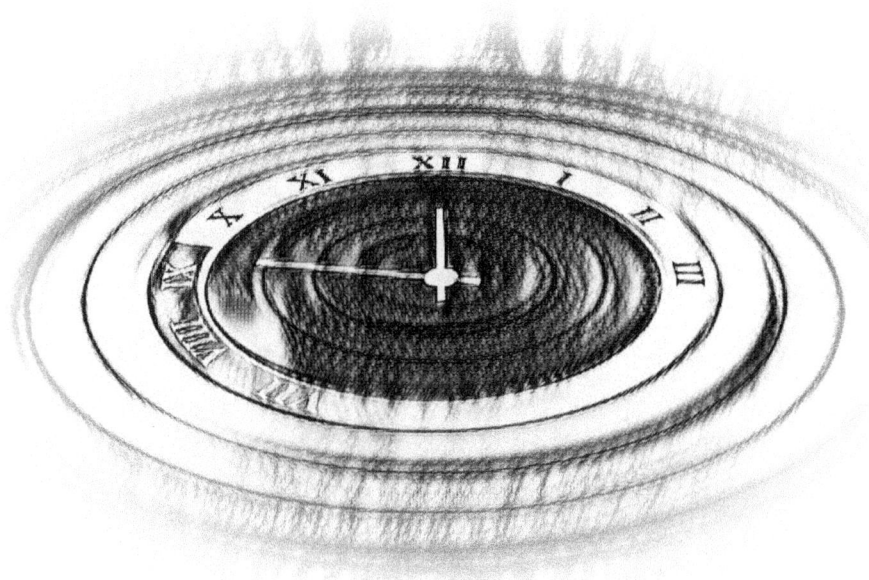

Dream One

Before I even opened my eyes in bed, I knew everything was different. And I don't mean because it was the first day after my fiftieth birthday. The first things I noticed were the bedsheets beneath me. They were soft, so incredibly soft. Silky rivers of satin carrying me down an endless river. I moved my legs back and forth and back and forth, getting that insatiable feeling of smoothness. That's when I opened my eyes, and yes, everything was different. The most exquisite, most expensive bedroom you could possibly imagine with solid cherry credenzas and headboards, velvet drapes, and a full technology package.

It worked.

I had just woken from a dream of the oddest kind. In the dream, I traveled back in time twenty years to see my thirty-year-old self. I visited my old house and waited outside till my younger self came home from work. Approaching the front porch, there was nothing he could have expected less than to see himself from twenty years into the future. After hurling a few phrases of shock and awe at me, and after I calmed my younger self down, we finally got to talking.

"How are we doing in the future?" young Marty asked.

"We're good. We're okay," I responded.

"Good, good," he nodded.

"We can be better though," I added.

"Oh? How do you mean?" young Marty asked me. How was I going to say this to my younger self? I was never exactly good at accepting advice. I always asked for it, oh jeez, always. From everyone and everything that can give it. But I never, ever took it. And I usually argued it to the death.

"Well, we could, ya know, be richer. Look, Marty," I began. "Let's be honest, I wasted a lot of time when I was your age. So much time, and so much money. What shows are you watching now?"

"Shows?" young Marty asked?

"Yeah, you know. TV shows."

213

I. Ashmawey

"Oh," young Marty thought. "House of Cards, Breaking Bad, Stranger Things, Walking Dead, Arrow, Game of Thro—"

"Yeah, yeah," I said. I waved to young Marty to join me on the porch, to which he obliged. "You see, that's kinda my point. There is nothing I hate more than wasting time." Then I paused for a second. "You know that of course, ha! Let me rephrase that, there is nothing *we* hate more than wasting time. But we still do. Anyway, have you ever wondered—ah, there I go again. You *have* wondered. I know you have."

"This is getting a tad annoying," young Marty said.

"Right, right, sorry. Okay, I'll just speak freely. Those shows, and the thousands of others, they completely take over your life. You know, episodic shows, that's one thing. Watch one episode, then watch the next one a year later, or not at all, and you're still fine. You just wanted to get some entertainment. But these serial shows, they take over. You live with the characters the writers created. They become your family, and you can't ever leave them. Until they leave you."

"Yeah, I've noticed that," young Marty said.

"Ah, anyway," I continued. "It's not just TV. Video games too. Sports! Oh the years of our lives we must have spent watching other people kick or throw a ball. Marty, we're spectators! We have to stop watching, and instead be the ones that others watch."

Young Marty was getting impatient. He stretched his legs and peered through the front window into the house. He missed his kids, he just wanted to get inside the house. "Yeah. Yeah, that sounds fine. I'll do that," young Marty responded. I furrowed my eyebrows, I can see clear through the lies.

"I'm fifty years old," I said. "In twenty years, we haven't progressed. Do you understand? We live in the same small house, we have the same job, and we have the same money problems. Are you understanding this?" This got young Marty's attention.

"But, I'm going for a promotion next month," young Marty said.

"And you'll get the promotion. And it'll give you some extra money. And then your expenses will grow to meet it. Every day of your life will be the same. Slowly, oh so slowly, you will start dying inside, Marty. Dying. You'll be an empty corpse with no soul," I said with vigor in my voice. My eyes were getting watery, I blinked quickly and repeatedly. Young Marty was lost in thought. Deep, deep thought.

Without averting his eyes from where they had been fixated across the street, he spoke slowly. "What should I do?" he asked.

"I can't tell you."

"You can't tell me?!" young Marty protested. "But I'm you. What on earth do you mean you can't tell me?"

"I can't. Success only comes to those who taste the struggle," I explained. "But I'll tell you this, and this is important: do not hold back. I'm going to repeat that. Do not hold back. You must sacrifice if you want success."

"What should I sacrifice?" young Marty asked.

"Whatever you feel is worthy of sacrificing to gain success," I responded.

And then I woke. And when I opened my eyes, my entire reality had changed. I was rich. I was successful. My dream wasn't actually a dream, it was real.

Dream Two

My second dream took place ten years after the first, on the night of my sixtieth birthday. It was just as random as the first and just as unexpected. The dream began with me swimming. I was fully immersed in water. I smelled chlorine, and felt the temperature of the water to be in the eighties… perfect. I must be in a pretty nice pool. When the dream commenced, I was in the middle of a perfect butterfly stroke. I pushed my head out of water and opened my eyes to see the most beautiful of mansions. Huge white pillars with steps that take leaps to go up. I saw gardens all around me. I continued swimming till I got out of the pool, and dried myself with a towel resting on one of the chaise longues.

I found a robe neatly placed near the pool; I put it on and pushed my hair back. Upon looking up, I saw an old man sitting in one of the gardens surrounding the pool. It was a butterfly garden with thousands of flowers of different kinds and different colors. The old man was frail with a slightly bent back. He had a walking stick and wore all white. His eyes were fixed on one of the flowers in front of him, or maybe all of them, or maybe none.

As I made my way to him, one thing became exceptionally clear: this man was me, but older. Once I realized this, my walk to him became more hastened. When his eyes met mine, he didn't seem surprised, almost as if he had been waiting for me. Waiting for decades. I joined him on the bench, overlooking some beautiful monarch butterflies.

"I'm glad we listened to each other," I said to older Marty.

"Listened?" he asked, so incredibly slow.

"Yeah, you know. About taking our life more seriously. Becoming a success," I explained. I looked around the gardens. They were so beautiful. "I mean, I'm pretty successful at sixty years old. I'm glad to see my success grows to unbound limits in the future." I took a deep breath and continued to look around. "I have so much to look forward to."

Older Marty didn't say anything. He also didn't show much facial expression. I guess when a person gets older, they simply show less emotion. Instead, he just nodded his head slowly, giving partial nods.

"Look, I know you can't tell me much about my future," I said to older Marty, "but tell me something!"

"What do you want to know?" he asked me.

"Well, this house! When did you buy it? How big is it?" I asked. Just as he was about to respond, I interrupted. "Is this your only house? Sorry, *our* only house?"

Older Marty took a deep breath and exhaled. It was almost as if he was sick of me, sick of himself twenty years ago. "Marty, this is one of seven homes."

"What?! This is amazing!" I looked around again at the mansion as if seeing it for the first time. "Older Marty, you have it made. You definitely have it made, my friend."

"I have things, yes," older Marty continued saying as he continued to nod his head slightly.

"Okay, I'm sorry. Just one more thing," I said. "Just tell me one more thing we have that I can look forward to."

Older Marty stood up very slowly. His back curved, his knees weak, his hair white as clouds. "Very well," he said. "You see, when you came to me decades ago, you used a tactic to persuade me. You used fear. You scared me into giving you, giving us, the future that you wanted. And so, going with your suggestion, I sacrificed for success. I sacrificed everything. As such...." his voice went silent for a second. "As such, Marty, I have seven homes. And all are empty. I have them all to myself, and no one to share them with." Older Marty patted my back and then began slowly walking away. "Enjoy looking forward to that."

34

The Affect of the Effect of Dreams
~based on a true story~

I. Ashmawey

Rachel was about to have the most dreadful car ride of her entire life. She was strong, always strong. Though her husband ran out on her during her pregnancy, she still found a way to pull through. She buckled her five-month-old son, Danny, into the car seat. She kissed his forehead, a kiss that lingered long enough for her to wipe a tear from her eye before getting into the driver's seat. She pushed her curly red hair back out of her eyes and regained her composure. Putting on her seatbelt felt like a pointless act. Why should she care about the seatbelt? For her safety? Who cared at that point? So what if she...

No.

None of that now.

No place for self-pity in this. Rachel had gone through hell before, and she'll do it again. And she'll come out the other side unscathed and unburned. But, let's be honest, no hell matched the fiery flames of what Rachel was going through in that moment. As she ritualistically drove home, she let her subconscious take over as her mind escaped to another land. A land filled with meadows and gardens where she and Danny could run and play from dawn till dusk. They would fall asleep under the stars and the next morning, wake up and immediately run again.

But that land was far, far away from her grasp. For Danny had been born with complete infant paralysis.

It wasn't polio. Actually, the doctors didn't know what it was, and so they couldn't cure him. It wasn't viral, but it also wasn't genetic. For one reason or another, young Danny was entirely paralyzed.

Rachel had just taken Danny to his final doctor visit. That visit when all the doctors agreed there was nothing more they could do. That visit when Rachel realized she had spent all the money she had, and didn't have, in hopes her son could walk again. That visit when she recognized yet *another* opinion wasn't going to better her chances of getting a *different* opinion. It was that visit, and it was the last one she would have. As far as she knew.

But Rachel was not the type to give into weakness. The day she got the letter from her husband saying he would not return to them was the same day she applied to jobs. It was the same day she bought six books on single parenting. It was also the same day she started looking into college investment plans. That's just the kind of person Rachel was.

Arriving at home, she took Danny out of the car seat and carried him inside. With every step she took, she thought about one thing: one day, this will not be normal. Right then, with Danny at five months old, it was perfectly fine for her to be carrying him into the house. At some age though, it wouldn't be. At some age, it was going to hit her, and hit her hard.

Walking into the house, she climbed up the stairs. She would have to move to a place without stairs. She went into Danny's bedroom and put him down on the bed. She lay next to him on the bed and cuddled him close. Babies are always peaceful when they're asleep. She looked across the room and saw all the toys Danny would never use. Stuffed animals, puzzles, toy cars, soccer balls.

How would she ever survive this?

Okay, you know what? One night. Rachel would allow herself one night of crying. One night to cry out every single tear she had inside her. Every single drop would leave her heart that night. She was allowed that much. And never again would she think of crying.

And so she did.

Rivers and streams flowed from her eyes. Sobbing shakes coupled with barbaric groans. Sounds and no sounds. Shakes and shivers and everything in between, all leaving her body like they were trapped inside for five months and finally had some freedom. And when she cried every cry, and made every sound, she closed her eyes and went back to Danny, holding him tight. She lay her head next to his, nose to nose. He was so small, so tiny, so... helpless.

Then Rachel did what she knew she probably should not do, but did anyway. She imagined young Danny living with full physical capabilities. At first, she allowed her imagination to start small, young Danny was crawling. And of course, if he was to crawl, he would be crawling to her. Rachel was on her knees, cheering him on to crawl faster. He did, and her arms were held wide, waiting for him to come close to her heart. Next, she imagined Danny a little bit older, around five or six years of age, bouncing on a trampoline. The smile on his face reached ear to ear. Next, he was a young teenager, hitting a home run in a school baseball game. He jumped up into the sky in cheer, then rounded the bases. His cap flying off his head, and his eyes narrowing in on Rachel, full of pride but looking for approval. And she gave it to him, with every ounce of love she had to offer.

But at some point in her imagining, Rachel drifted off to sleep. And somehow, she knew she was asleep. It wasn't because of how things looked, but rather how they felt. She was cold, but there was no wind. She was standing somewhere outdoors. There was a spotlight shining on her, everything else was pitch dark.

Beneath her bare feet, a thin blanket of white snow. She crushed the untouched snowflakes with the tips of her toes as her chest shuddered, letting out the last bit of warmth inside her.

Slowly, the figure of a man approached her. Wearing a long, black coat and black fedora, she couldn't see his face. Not because it was hidden, but because being in a dream state restricted her from having the full freedom to see everything she wanted. The man had both hands behind his back. He slowly brought them both out in front of him. In his left hand, he held a cloth bag. On it, was drawn a dollar symbol in green, just like in cartoons. In his right hand, he carried an infant. Laying in his palm, she immediately noticed it was Danny. She let out a short scream and tried to reach out to him, but she couldn't budge. She was completely paralyzed.

"Your son," the man said, in a voice deeper than echoes in a cave, "or one hundred million dollars." He held out both his hands closer to her.

"My son!" Rachel screamed. Not a second of hesitation in her voice. She wanted to reach out to Danny and take him back, but she still wasn't able to. *This must be what Danny feels*, she thought to herself. *He must want to reach out to me, but can't.*

"Are you certain?" the man asked. "He's paralyzed. He can never give you the love you seek. He will never be what you look for in a son." That made Rachel fume. How dare he? How dare he speak that way of her son, her life, her love? What does he know about what she wants?

In a second, she broke out of what was holding her back. She leaped at the man's hand and took hold of Danny. She held him close, oh so close. Squeezing him as hard as she could without breaking his fragile bones.

Then she woke.

Rachel opened her eyes, and found that she was, in fact, squeezing Danny while lying on his bed. Tears flew from her eyes and fell on his soft, warm face.

Then...

In a second...

As if from a dream...

Danny rolled over to his stomach and crawled on the bed.

35

Ganglionic Potentiality

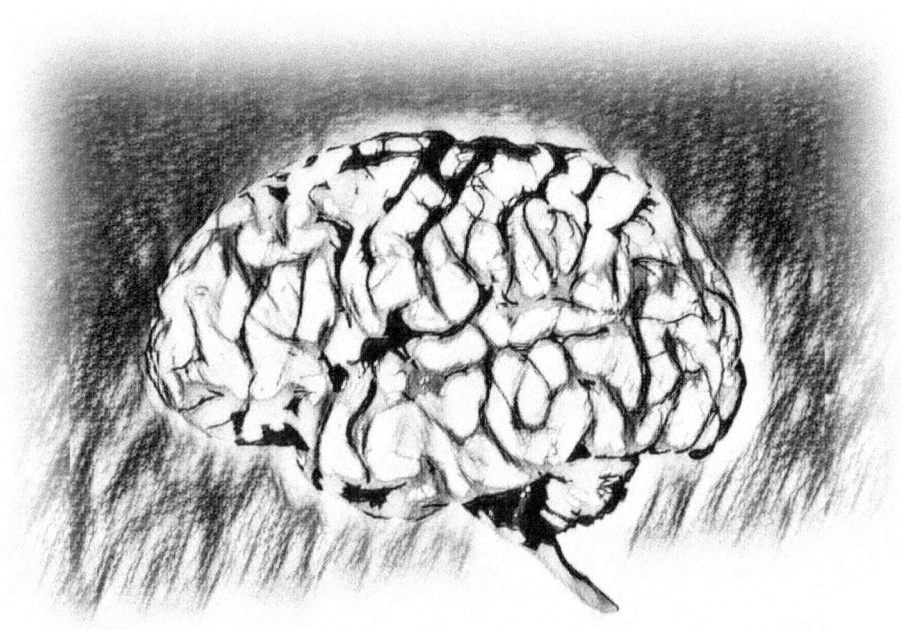

K enneth Serling's death occurred because of a question. One question sparked a chain of events that would change his entire life.

As a young boy, Kenneth's mother would always warn him of his curiosity. "Curiosity killed the... I don't remember. It killed something," she would tell him. That didn't have much of an effect on young Kenneth. His days were spent between exploring the deepest depths of the forest beyond his backyard, or in the most intricate circuit boards of any technology he could find. Kenneth was always looking where no one else was, often times in a dangerous fashion. "You're going to kill yourself someday," his mother would say. He didn't understand why he would ever want to kill himself, there was too much to explore! Kenneth would just push aside his long, silky brown hair from in front of his thick glasses and continue on with his exploration.

In his late teens, a vibrant Kenneth Serling sat in a college neurology course. The professor was discussing the effects of Chronic Traumatic Encephalopathy. The causes, symptoms, signs, etc. Something was bothering Kenneth though. A question. One he wondered about as a child, and because of it, he chose this line of study. And thus far in his courses, it's been completely skipped over. Kenneth raised his hand in the lecture.

"Sir?" he began. "Where are memories stored?"

The professor, a plump man in his late sixties, thick glasses and a naive smile, was taken back by the question. And while the question had nothing to do with that day's lecture, the professor was not someone to ever turn a student down. Especially the curious ones.

"Well," the professor started, "I... I... I think you're referring to brain cells. As I'm sure you've covered in your studies, memories are formed and recalled when neighboring brain cells send chemical communications across the synapses that connect them. Each time a memory is recalled, the connection is reactivated and strengthened."

"Right, I get that," Kenneth responded, rather disappointed. "But I mean, where is it actually physically stored? Like, when you talk about computers, the answer is pretty explicit. It's magnetic fields. Data is stored digitally in the form of tiny magnetized regions, each region representing a bit, one or zero. I can point to a hard drive and show you exactly where the data is stored, and how. But with the brain—"

"Mr... Serling, correct?" the professor asked. Kenneth nodded. "You're looking to make comparisons between a human organ and a machine. We don't have the same level of detail on the brain as we do a computer. Perhaps it's because we created the computer. I'm not sure. If I can bring your attention back to this diagram here..." And with that, the professor went back to his course.

The question never left Kenneth's mind, however. Not for a moment in all the years to come. In fact, Kenneth Serling made it his life's mission to answer the simple question: where is memory stored? To conduct his research, he began with the only avenue we currently have to access memories, our brain. Wherever memories were stored, we knew for fact that the brain had access to them. What exactly happened to the brain when synapses between neurons were fired?

It was twenty years later that Kenneth had the answer. And his public announcement to the academic community did not phase well at first. For the results of his experiments were entirely unexpected.

"Our brains can access memories," he said in his famous lecture, "because our brains... can access the past." This was met by loud murmurs throughout the lecture hall. One person even chuckled out loud. At first, people thought it was a joke, as if Kenneth was saying the obvious. Obviously, our brains access the past, that's what a memory is. But Kenneth was speaking literally. He meant our brains can, in reality, travel through time to the past, and that is what happened every time we recalled a memory. And once Kenneth presented his evidence, a deafening silence swept over the room. He had explicitly proven that recalling memories is, in fact, a mental astral projection—a time travel—into the actual past.

Within weeks, a slew of neurological questions were answered. What happens when one induces a neurological synapse firing? It causes the mind to travel to the past. What is a synapse firing? It is, in every essence of the word, time travel. And most importantly, for Kenneth at least, where are memories stored? They aren't. Memories don't exist. The past exists, same as the present.

Kenneth had answered his question. And if any amongst you know, it is an amazing feeling for one to have a goal, especially one so close to impossible, and then fulfill it. Few moments are more rewarding. But, being Kenneth Serling, he immediately had another goal. And as if the first one was not difficult enough, his second goal was mathematically and scientifically proven by his peers to be impossible. Funny how Kenneth worked though, that only made him insist upon it more. And just to rub it in everyone's face, Kenneth held another press conference just to announce his impossible goal.

"Ladies and gentlemen, thank you all for being here. I asked you all to come so that I may present to you my next project. It is one that has already garnered some negative feedback and attention. My next project, the one I have called Ganglionic Potentiality, is an effort to harness the energy used by our brains in the process of traveling to the past, and transfer it to our physical bodies."

The reactions were... expected. It was not a time when hanging for heresy was commonplace in the scientific community. But if they could revive such methods for one person, they would have picked Kenneth Serling. He now wanted to time travel? And how? Through his brain? The understanding that recalling memories was actually a mental travel through time was still brand new. The ink hadn't even dried on the research. And here was Kenneth, announcing that he was going to fully understand the process our brains go through, to the point that he will harness that energy and transfer it to his physical body.

It was another twenty years later that a sixty-year-old Kenneth sat in the basement of his house where he had a fully functional lab. A place where he had been tinkering for decades. Papers stacked up to the ceiling, gizmos and gadgets scattered all around, and a constant, incessant whirring sound came from a machine at the far end of the room. The machine looked like a hybrid between a coffin and a standing MRI. Except, unlike an MRI, this machine had a strong, metallic exterior. Scrawled across the top in permanent marker, Kenneth had written "GPM" and beneath it, "Ganglionic Potentiality Machine."

Kenneth had been working now for months without a break. He was so close, he knew he was just days away. As he tinkered away on a circuit board in front of him, he had to constantly push his silky gray hair off his thick glasses and wipe his sweaty forehead to keep the heavy drops from falling onto his work. He remembered his mother. "You're going to kill yourself someday," she would say. She was wrong. He was going to change the world with his invention.

"Kenneth?" a voice from behind him spoke. A voice so familiar... too familiar. Only one person had this voice. He spun around to find an older, hunched over Kenneth Serling standing in front of him. His hair mostly gone, his skin wrinkled, his overall body almost transparent, slowly becoming more opaque. Like he was coming into existence. "You've succeeded Kenneth. You've succeeded."

Kenneth's eyes shot wide open. Talk about success. Talk about accomplishment. He had not yet even fully completed his machine but was already seeing the fruits of his labors. He knew, in that moment, that he would succeed. Something that no human being had ever experienced before in history.

"It ... will work," Kenneth said, to himself, and to Old Kenneth.

"It will, Kenneth. It will," Old Kenneth spoke with slight pride in his voice. He slowly dragged his feet over to Kenneth with great difficulty. He was so old, Kenneth guessed somewhere between ninety and ninety-five. "I know what kind of pride you are feeling right now."

Kenneth, still staring with his mouth hung open, had only a quantum of a smile. He was still in a state of shock and amazement. "Yes. Yes, I believe if anyone does, it would be you," he responded.

"Which makes what I am about to say extremely difficult," Old Kenneth began. Even the hint of the smile Kenneth wore quickly dissipated. "I'm sorry, Kenneth. I apologize to myself and to you. But you must cease this project."

As much as Kenneth's face was serious and stern, he couldn't help but chuckle. Just one quick chuckle before going directly back to stone-cold seriousness. "Cease the project? You must have a tremendously interesting explanation, old man."

"I do," Old Kenneth said. "But sadly, I cannot share it with you. I can only tell you that our project will change the world. It will." Kenneth smiled again at hearing this. "But then it will destroy the world. Kenneth, I'm not your enemy. I am you, and I have your best interest in mind the same as you have your own best interest in mind. If I was anyone else, I would understand suspicion. But the fact that I am the one telling you this should immediately make you realize that you should take it seriously. Kenneth, you must shut down your project."

Kenneth put his head down. He shook it slowly back and forth, and then furiously. His lips curled in an angry growl. "No, old man. Nothing in hell will make me stop this project. Whatever mistake you made, I will avoid it. You can either help me fix whatever you did, or be useless."

Old Kenneth nodded his head. "I knew this would be your reaction, of course. All I had to do was think of myself at your age." And without a single notice, Old Kenneth pulled out a gun and shot Kenneth in the chest.

They both immediately fell to their knees, gasping for breath.

"I'm sorry, young lad," Old Kenneth said, barely able to let out a sound. "I'm saving the world."

Kenneth's eyes were shot wide open. Pain, amazement, shock, all ran through his veins. "Mom was right," he said. "I'm going to kill myself." Kenneth's eyes closed. Old Kenneth quickly disappeared.

36

A Halloween Carol

I. Ashmawey

U sually it was only the children who looked forward to Halloween. But no matter his age, Peter Bradbury always loved bidding summer farewell. To Peter, there was nothing more amazing than the ancient tradition of Samhain. Nothing brought more happiness than the slew of orange and black, with a touch of green and purple. The smell of pumpkin and cinnamon filling every store, every street, and every home. The silhouette shape of a witch on her broomstick, the perfectly rounded and curved shape of pumpkins with huge, thick stems, twisted and turned, the almost medicinal shape of a skeleton and being able to see through the ribs; every image incited a certain feeling of thrill and giddiness! The sounds of ghosts wooo-ing, and witches cackling, and the Ghostbusters theme, and Monster Mash singing, all flew through the air, traveling from town to town and radio to radio. Peter enjoyed everything more than any and every child on the block. And he didn't hide it either.

Everything was different in Halloween.

And that's what Peter loved, even at the ripe age of seventy-five. Everything was different. It was as if the world was experiencing escapism from itself, transporting to an alternate reality that is much prettier and far more exciting. Halloween was perfect. Except, there wasn't enough of it. And Peter Bradbury knew he did not have many more left. He was getting older, and his arthritis was not improving. Still, he tried to enjoy every day as best as he could. Retirement wasn't exactly what Peter thought it would be. The time... grew. It multiplied. Peter had worked as a successful accountant for fifty-five years. He had saved up just enough for retirement and had initially planned on living life to the fullest with all the free time he had. But health got in the way. And as it was, Peter was spending his days counting down till October came.

There wasn't much where Peter lived. But the one thing he always wished his small town of Troy, Michigan had was a haunted house. And not just for Halloween, but all year round. Since he was young, he and his friends would drive for hours to the nearest haunted house all the way in Grand Rapids. For the two hours there, they would complain about how far the drive was, and for the two hours back, they would revel in how amazing the haunt was. Maybe someday they'd have one closer to home.

So it was this cold, haunted night, All Hallows Eve. Peter had prepared the Halloween candy and arranged it in the witch's pots, he laid out his vampire costume on the chair at his wife's vanity, and most importantly, personally turned on every lit up decoration, indoor and outdoor. Sure there were automatic timers, but where was the fun in that?

Getting into bed, looking up at the handful of lit up plastic jack-o-lanterns in the bookshelf in his bedroom, and the black spider web spreading from the mantel above the door to the closet, and the skeleton hung by the window, Peter felt such an overwhelming happiness. One so strong, he could not get himself to fall asleep. Lying there, eyes wide, Peter began to sing to himself in a whisper.

"Five little pumpkins sitting on a gate. First one said 'Oh my, it's getting late!' Second one said, 'There are witches in the air.' The third one said 'But we don't care!' The fourth one said 'Let's run and run and run.' The fifth one said…"

"I'm ready for some fun!" a voice spoke. Peter jolted in his place, shaking the bed. He looked over at his wife and found her still softly snoring. It couldn't have been her. The voice was deep and echoing. It spoke so slowly, enunciating every single syllable.

"Who's there?" Peter asked with a stutter in his voice.

"Why, it's Bram," the voice spoke again. At that point, old Peter was on his feet. His frail hand was shaking as he tried grabbing for a flashlight, which he was barely able to grasp.

"Bram… who? Where are you?" Then Peter flung around the moment he heard footsteps behind him. And there stood Bram.

A man wearing a black suit. His shirt was striped black and white, as well as his socks. He wore a short top hat with a green ribbon wrapped around it. He also carried a pitchfork in his right hand. None of that was too off-putting. Oh, except the fact that his head was a jack-o-lantern. And maybe also that he appeared out of nowhere and sounded like death.

Peter screamed. He yelled and screamed and tried to run away, but he couldn't. He was frozen in place. He called out to his wife, nothing. He looked over to her and what he saw scared him more than he was already scared; he saw himself laying in bed. Bram happily observed Peter's confusion with a jack-o-lantern-ey smile on his ever-familiar visage. Eventually, Peter stopped screaming. Bram's smile didn't dissipate as Peter attempted to finally catch his breath.

"You're a good screamer, Peter Bradbury," Bram said, moving his three, perfectly shaped teeth. "You can tell it comes from your soul."

"What in heaven's name is going on!?" Peter screamed in confusion.

"It's rather simple, Peter Peter Bo-Peter. My name is Bram."

"Yes, you said that already!"

"I'm a ghost, so to speak," Bram explained.

"A... ghost?"

"Correct. I guess you can say the Ghost of Halloween past," Bram said. His pumpkin smile grew a tad. Peter started getting disoriented. The ghost of Halloween past? What on earth was this pumpkin-headed, funny-dressed, smiling man talking about? "Look, Peter Bradbury. You know your Dickens, I've seen your library. I want to take you on a little trip."

"Well, now hold on a minute! A trip to what?! I'm extremely generous," Peter protests.

"Yes, yes you are."

"Okay then! Why are we even doing this then? I have a great life. I'm kind, courteous, and usually very humble if I'm not defending myself to a ghost," Peter said. Bram let out a huge laugh. He liked this guy.

"True, true. Peter, what I want to show you is not something you would necessarily know is a problem. Actually, most everyone does not. Give me your hand, Peter." Bram held out his left hand, draped in a thin black glove. Peter looked at his wife, then at his sleeping body right next to her. This was a dream, it was fine. And, he supposed, the point of dreams was to be adventurous. He took Bram's hand. As soon as his skin touched the fabric of Bram's glove, Peter felt... nothing.

He looked up to Bram questioningly, and then noticed they had transported somewhere else entirely! Looking around, Peter saw all things that he loved. Cobwebs, sheets on furniture, broken tables, peeling wallpaper, gaps in the floorboards, holes in the walls, a lonesome chandelier with broken strings of crystals, spiders scurrying into their holes in the walls, gloomy staircases, and old portraits. Peter knew exactly where he was. He was in a haunted house. He didn't care to ask any questions, he was far too excited! He began slowly walking up to the second floor, cringing at each creak on the old warped stairs. Halfway up, a shadow loomed at the corner of his eyesight. Peter froze, the scent of a phantom perfume filled the air. Looking down, he saw skeletons all over the floor. All that was in sight was damp.

The haunted house continued, throwing surprise after surprise, haunt after haunt, fear after fear, it was all so delicious. Even though Peter was a professional after so many years, he still let out a number of unexpected screams. At times, he was genuinely scared for his life. Some of the haunts were so realistic, he had difficulty convincing himself they were fake.

As he walked out the front door of the haunted house with Bram, letting out hearty laughs right and left, Peter rested his hand on Bram's shoulder. "Oh, wow!" Peter said, still catching his breath. "Thank you so much for that. Thank you. That was truly amazing. Okay, now that that's said and done, do you care to explain to me why you gave me this wonderful treat?" Bram didn't say anything, his smile never swayed. Instead, he just pointed his pitch fork to the haunted house they had just stepped out of. He pointed up, above the front door. Peter raised his gaze, and what he saw took away all the happiness from his heart. If you would have asked him just yesterday, he would have told you that of course, such a sight would make him happy. But it didn't. He felt the deepest, darkest feeling of gloom in his chest. Like a hollow, painful emptiness that made it hard to breath, above the front door hung a sign that read "Peter Bradbury's House of Horrors."

The best haunted house Peter had been to in decades was, in fact, his own. But it wasn't, for he never decided to grasp that dream and make it a reality. "What is this, Bram?" Peter asked.

"It's Hell, Peter," Bram said softly. "Hell is meeting the person you could have become. Normally, one meets that person on their last day on earth. But you've been given a glimpse. And how lucky you are to have been given that."

"I thought I was happy," Peter said somberly. He thought of his wife, his kids, and his years of being an accountant.

Good God. He hated retirement. And his work was never happy, and therefore neither was his life.

"You and I both know the truth, Peter Bradbury," Bram said. "Happy Halloween."

And with that, Peter opened his eyes. He was in his bed, next to his wife. He looked out the window and saw the sun just peaking over the horizon. It was so early on this cold Halloween morning.

Just early enough.

For Peter had a lot of work to do before nightfall. And suddenly, he had such a surge of energy.

37

The Rumored Love of Scarlett Johansson

I. Ashmawey

Alex Richardson had been in love with Becky Rostom since kindergarten. And trust me, she was worth loving. When he had his first fight at school, he got hurt pretty bad. And to make matters worse, he was the only one to get in trouble. Sitting in the principal's office, waiting for his fate to be determined, he was ecstatic to find Becky sneaking into the office to give him a kiss on the cheek and tell him everything would be alright. What an amazing girl.

They were neighbors, spending summers exploring wilderness together and winters building snowmen together. As they grew older, their friendship continued. Friendship for Becky, infatuation for Alex. Then came middle school, when boys turned into men and girls turned into forces of nature. Becky was always kind to Alex. But, let's be blunt, he became a nerd and she became a princess. If he got beat up less, it was because of her. If anyone ever spoke to him, it was because of her. If anything remotely good ever happened to Alex throughout those years, it was always because of Becky Rostom. High school and college were much of the same. She had boyfriends by the flock, Alex played video games by the clock. In college, Becky studied fashion while Alex studied computer graphics. As luck would have it, or as he carefully planned and plotted, Alex ended up working for a small computer design firm owned by Becky's Dad.

Now, Becky's Dad absolutely loved Alex. He had always loved him since he was a kid. Smart, kind-hearted, dependable, Alex was everything anyone would love. And so one fateful day, Becky's Dad called Alex into his office.

"Have a seat, Alex," he said as he took his glasses off and placed them on his desk. "I'm going to be very frank with you son." Alex nodded. "I know you love my daughter."

Alex's face turned red and his eyes shot open like baseballs sticking out of his face. He shook his head furiously. "What! Oh my God, Mr. Rostom. How could—"

"Shut up, son," Mr. Rostom interrupted. "It's clear as day to the blindest of men. You've loved her since the moment your family moved into the neighborhood. Anyway, I've decided I'm going to help you win her heart." That got Alex's attention. Suddenly his face went from red to all shades of hopefulness. "And before you ask me why, let me tell you. I hate the guys she's dating. Hate, hate, hate them. Selfish, irresponsible brats most of them. And every time, her little heart gets broken. What kind of a Dad would I be if I didn't step in?" he asked. Alex just shrugged his shoulders, he was still in shock. Did he really have a chance at being with the girl he's loved his entire life?

"Anyways son, I have a plan. But as I'm working on it, I need you to… Jesus…" Mr. Rostom said as he put his glasses back on and looked at Alex up and down. "You have some work to do, don't you?"

"Sorry, what do you mean sir?" Alex asked. Mr. Rostom didn't respond. Instead, he hit his intercom button.

"Sally, come in here please," he said to his secretary. Moments later, a young lady in her twenties, roughly same age as Alex, came into the room with blonde hair comfortably styled and fashionable thick-framed glasses. "Sally, do me a favor. Actually, do Alex a favor. Can you take him shopping please?"

"What?" Alex asked.

"Use the company card. Just…" Mr. Rostom waved his hands in the air in front of Alex. "Just do something here. Make him over entirely." Mr. Rostom turned to Alex. "By the time you get back, my boy, I'll have some good stuff for you."

This would be a good time to describe to you what Alex Richardson looked like. Alex was a skinny young man. His light brown hair was longer than average and always messy. The tips were curled in a million little directions. He wore thick glasses with frames that were leopard colored. His pants: thick beige corduroy. Everyday, all year long. He always wore flannel shirts and for some reason always had one side tucked in and the other tucked out. His face was shaven, but never cleanly.

The man who came back into Mr. Rostom's office a few hours later however was a different human being. Contacts in his eyes, hair gelled to the side and neatly cut, dark blue jeans, clean white button down shirt, and a nice shave. Sally took a bow to Mr. Rostom, proud of her accomplishment. She got a small bonus that day.

"Okay, okay, sit down, son!" Mr. Rostom said giddily. "Man, you look great! Okay, take a look… at this!" Mr. Rostom turned his computer screen to show the oddest thing Alex had ever seen. It was a selfie photo of Alex sitting at a romantic Italian restaurant, sharing a plate of spaghetti… with Scarlett Johansson.

"Holy… selfies…" Alex spit out.

"Isn't it great? I have a bunch!" Mr. Rostom laughed out loud. He scrolled through more pictures of Alex and Scarlett Johansson. Getting an ice cream together, walking through a garden hand in hand, and the sorts. All the photos were selfie style and all of them… real!

"Mr. Rostom, what on earth is going on here?" Alex asked in shock.

"These photos are going to get you Becky's heart, son. Not only that, I've already leaked them all online! The whole world has seen them by now."

"How on earth!"

"They're so good, right? I made them all myself. No one, and I mean no one, could tell they're doctored. Now, here's what's going to happen. You're going to come over to the house tonight. Becky is having a small get together for her fashion clients. I'll tell the family that we have some business to discuss. You're going to bring your laptop bag, and these photos are going to casually and conveniently fall out of your bag. Becky's going to see them. And like any normal person would, she's going to feel jealous. You always want what you can't have, right?" Alex nodded unsurely. "Right?! I mean, are you happy seeing Becky with other guys?" Alex shook his head vigorously. "Okay, then. Becky will notice you in a completely different light. She'll become more interested in you, and sure enough, fall in love with you. You'll eventually have to explain that you will have to let down Ms. Johansson softly, since you would prefer Becky. And what kind of girl wouldn't be thrilled to be picked over Scarlett Johansson, huh?"

Mr. Rostom had a plan. It was an idiotically stupid plan (who carried physical photos these days anyway?). There was no way Alex was going to be able to pull it off and he knew that, but it was a plan. And that was more than Alex ever had. So he agreed, in hopes that Mr. Rostom would do the majority of the talking. Alex and Mr. Rostom spent the rest of the day making up stories. How he and Scarlett met, how they fell in love, how long they've been together, etc. By the time they both got to Mr. Rostom's house, they had begun to believe the stories themselves!

It was a full house, fashion clients from all over the state had come to mingle. Alex clutched his laptop bag closely under his armpit and made his way through the crowd till he found Becky. She embraced him with a big hug.

"Alex! What a surprise! God, I'm always so happy to see you!" she yelled out with the warmest of smiles that melted his heart. "Come, come, let me introduce you to some of these people." She locked arms with him and walked him to the back yard. What an amazing feeling it was to lock arms with her, Alex was floating on cloud nine. He was introduced to so many people, it was impossible to remember a single name. After all, all he really cared about was being around Becky. And her introducing him to people gave him a feeling of... belonging to her.

"Oh, and this is my favorite client of all! And I'm honored to call her a friend! Alex, meet Scarlett Johansson."

A deep, heavy, deafening boom completely drowned out every single sound.

Scarlett... who?

All Alex could hear was his own heartbeat. And sure enough, the woman in front of them, moving in extra slow motion, turned around. Her perfect hair flew oh so slowly. And just as her face came into view, Alex almost fainted. There she was, Scarlett Johansson. In all her perfection. He was done for. Wait! Maybe he wasn't. He took a deep breath, trying desperately to regain his hearing. As Becky went on and on to Scarlett about how long she's known him, Alex tried thinking of anything he could do next to salvage the situation.

Dammit, Mr. Rostom! Why didn't you pick Megan Fox instead?! Okay, I haven't said anything yet. I'll keep the photos to myself. We'll have to think of another plan. I'll just have to—

"Oh, I know Alex. How have you been?" Scarlett asked.

Holy crap.

"What! You two know each other?!" Becky screamed.

"Oh yeah. We've been friends for... oh jeez... a couple years now, right Alex?" Scarlett said with an angelic smile. Alex just stood there.

You idiot! At least nod your head!

So he nodded his head.

"Yeah, it's kind of a long story," Scarlett explained. Just then, someone came and pulled Becky away.

"One sec, you two. I'll be right back," Becky said, still astonished. And there stood Alex Richardson and Scarlett Johansson. Alex, his heart pounding and his mind racing. Scarlett, calm as a millpond.

"Excuse me, Ms. Johansson?" Alex started. That's when Scarlett started cracking up.

"Oh Alex. Trust me, you're not the first nor the last to fake a relationship with me to get someone else's attention." She continued laughing.

Good God! She knows!

"Don't worry, I won't say anything," she explained. Then her face got a bit more serious. "Just, please, for your own sake, be yourself. If she's going to like you because of me, I can guarantee you it'll be short-lived." Alex looked down to the ground, she was right. Scarlett Johansson was right, as difficult as it still was to believe the situation he was in and who he was talking to.

"You're right, ma'am," he said.

"Ma'am? Making me feel like a grandma," she joked.

"Sorry. But yes, you're right. Sorry, this whole thing was her Dad's idea. He felt that if I used pictures of you and ... the pictures!"

Just then, Becky came running up to them holding up her cell phone, showing them a photo. Her face was stern and a vain was about to pop on her forehead.

"Oh... crap."

38

Jane and Sherlock:
The Case of the Frenemy

I. Ashmawey

Jane and Sherlock

Brompton Middle School, San Francisco, California. In a busy school hallway, Jane Watson, a well-dressed and confident thirteen year old hangs around the lockers passing out 'Vote for Jane' pins.

"Vote for Jane for class President! Vote for me please, I stick up for any good cause no matter what!" If ever a girl loved her school, it would be Jane Watson. Her school, her city, her town, her home.

"Why should I vote for you?" a random student asks her as he takes a pin. And not asking in a nice way, either.

"Because I care about the well-being of every single student in this school. And it's an honest, genuine care," she responds confidently. The student looks at the pin, then tosses it back to her rudely, and walks off. No matter though, Jane's smile doesn't falter. She opens her locker. But while pulling out books, a strange noise comes from... somewhere... but where?

And out of thin air, appears Sherlock Holmes. Roughly her same age with dark messy hair, standing there camouflaged into the lockers. He turns to look at Jane who is screaming in his face.

"Who are you? Where did you come from?? You scared me half to death!" she yells at him.

"You can't scare someone to death," he responds in his British accent. "That's a guilt tactic perpetrated by mothers."

"And why are you dressed like a locker? Where did you come from?" she continues. That's when Sherlock whips out a mini spiral notebook from the inside pocket of his tweed blazer and scribbles furiously. Jane tries unsuccessfully to peek. "What... um... what are you writing?"

Without taking his eyes off his notepad, Sherlock responds. "Apparently, Americans are nosy and have little respect for privacy."

"Are you wearing tweed? And a derby hat?? No seriously, can we talk about this derby hat?" she asks.

"No." Sherlock rolls his eyes and puts away his journal. "Yes, obviously I'm a new student here. And, also obviously, I'm from England. And my name is Sherlock

Holmes."

"Oh! Well, would you like me to give you a tour of the school?" she asks excitedly. Sherlock takes off his camouflage costume of the lockers.

"Since you're one of the smartest students at this school, and you're particularly smart in history, it would be wise for me to accept a history lesson on the school from you," Sherlock says, rather quickly. "Moreover, you clearly care about this place since you're running for student council, and I also understand why you were scrutinizing my wardrobe since you meticulously make your own clothes."

Jane is dumbfounded. "How do you know all that, mystery boy?"

"It's as simple as the paper in your hand. A history test graded with one hundred and five percent. The callus on your middle finger which indicates your studious nature. And your handmade bracelets and skirt that have your initials sewn in. Not very well-sewn either."

"Wow! Can I say wow? I'm going to say wow. Wow," Jane says with a smile on her face.

"Just say it already. Good lord," Sherlock says. Just then, the bell rings. "Oh thank God, take me to class." Jane disappointedly nods. Her fun tour would have to wait. Instead, she begins walking him to class.

"So, Sherlock. As you know, I'm running for Student Council president. I'd love to have your vote."

"Why?"

Jane pulls out her recorded response. "Well, because I care about our school! I have great plans to fix our problems and I'd be a great representative of our school at the International Student Council Convention later this year."

"I don't vote. Sorry." And with that, Sherlock walks into the classroom. Jane, befuddled, follows behind.

"Well, who do we have here?" Mr. Malloy, their teacher, asks.

"Mr. Malloy, this is a new student, Sherlock Holmes," Jane says.

"Hello, Sherlock. You mind introducing yourself to the class?" Mr. Malloy asks.

"I do."

Mr. Malloy responds, rather annoyed. "Well, do it anyway, please."

Sherlock rolls his eyes. "My name is Sherlock Holmes. None of you should ever need to impede your consciousness onto my own." Jane buries her face in her hands.

"Delightful, Mr. Holmes," Mr. Malloy responds. "Let's begin with today's lesson. Hydrogen peroxide and potassium iodide. We're going to cover chapter twenty, and for homework, you'll be reading chapter twenty-one."

"Excuse me, Mr. Malloy, is it?" Sherlock interjects.

"Yes, Mr. Holmes."

"You can't assign homework," Sherlock says. Mr. Malloy looks confused as ever. Sherlock decides to elaborate. "Well, teachers assign homework without asking permission from students. What's worse, they punish students if they don't do it. But if they do their homework, they get nothing. Simply the absence of punishment. The motivation for doing homework thusly becomes to avoid punishment, and therefore, is torturing and unconstitutional."

A long awkward pause follows. Mr. Malloy squints his eyes and faces Sherlock like a western standoff.

"Mr. Holmes," Mr. Malloy starts. "While I wholeheartedly disagree with you, due to your eloquent speech, no homework tonight." The class erupts in cheer! All the students get up and start clapping for Sherlock who sits back in his chair, not amused. A bunch of them hoist an annoyed Sherlock on their shoulders. As they cheer, one student yells out...

"I'm nominating Sherlock Holmes for Student Council President!" Jane, hearing this, is in utter disbelief. She runs after the crowd carrying Sherlock as he yells at them.

"How can you nominate Sherlock? He's only been here for one day and doesn't know anything about the school!" she screams.

"He knows how to cancel our homework!" Another uproar of cheer. Sherlock finally gets himself down and walks away from the crowd. Nothing is worse than a crowd for Sherlock. As he walks away, at the other end of the hallway, a distraught and upset Jane sits on a bench. She worked so incredibly hard on her campaign, and not for selfish reasons, but because she genuinely cares about the school. It doesn't take her long to decide what she will do next. If Sherlock has gained fame, and the students love him, then he should win. Students need a Student Council president that they love, one they can confide in. That's the whole point of Student Council, isn't it?

Jane would vote for Sherlock.

Meanwhile, around the corner and in a small hallway, Sherlock runs into his older brother, Mycroft.

"Becoming famous so fast, are we Sherlock?" Mycroft asks.

"Mycroft, are you stalking me?" Sherlock asks.

"Oh, I wouldn't dare. Come sit with me," Mycroft motions to a small bench.

"Oh goodness, a talk from the older brother. How dreadful," Sherlock complains.

"Sherlock, do you remember Toby?"

"Toby?" Sherlock squints his eyes. "Of course I remember Toby. Goodness, I miss that wonderful dog. I do hope he's okay in England without us."

"Oh he's doing wonderful, I'm sure. Do you remember though when our neighbor Mrs. Hudson first met him?"

"How could I forget?" Sherlock says. "She immediately fell to her knees and gave him the biggest hug I've ever seen someone give. I suppose, with the loss of her husband, she really needed Toby, didn't she?"

"Yes. Yes, she did. But it wasn't just her that needed him. He needed her as well," Mycroft adds. "Let's be honest, Sherlock. We were both too busy for Toby. Sure, when we got him we were all very excited indeed. But it took only three days for us to be bored of him and go back to our normal lives. Toby was bored. He needed Mrs. Hudson just as much as she needed him. That's why we decided to give him up to her." Sherlock listens in silence. Mycroft gives him a second and then gets up slowly. He pats Sherlock on the shoulder as he walks away.

The next day in class, Sherlock sits quietly as he thinks to himself before Mr. Malloy interrupts his contemplation.

"As you know, we have an exam next week and I'm not sure how much of the material any of you understand since I haven't assigned homework for a few days, thanks to Mr. Holmes." The entire class erupts in cheer, once again. Jane smiles to herself.

Sherlock stands up. "Mr. Malloy. There have been many studies and with only rare exceptions, the relationship between homework and student success in life was positive and statistically significant," Sherlock says.

"Really, now?" Mr. Malloy questions.

"Yes, sir. After all, how else can positive reinforcement happen if not with homework? I was a fool to ever suggest it be eliminated." The entire class boos him and tells him to sit down.

"Now class. Calm down, calm down, please. Quiet!!" Mr. Malloy screams. Sherlock sits back down in his seat. Jane eyes him, confused. The second the bell rings, Sherlock leaves class first and heads to the voting booths. Jane tries to catch up with him but gets blocked by other students. During the next hour, all the students in the school cast their votes proudly. Later that day, the cafeteria is set up for a school assembly to announce the winners. Sherlock sees Jane sitting in one of the rows. He walks up to her.

"Is this seat taken?" he asks.

"Only if you plan to sit there," Jane responds with a smile. Sherlock makes himself comfortable. "Oh, by the way. I got you something." Jane pulls out a small package from her bag. "I saw this and it reminded me of you."

"You got me a gift even though I'm your competition?"

"Well, the challenge is always good. Anyway, you're going to win this election. And as long as we remain friends, that's all I care about. Oh, by the way, in class earlier today, about the homework, why did you change your..."

"Alright, boys and girls!" the Principal interrupts on her microphone. "It's been a wonderful race! But every race must have an end. This year's class president is... Ms. Jane Watson!"

Jane's face becomes flushed. She can't believe her ears. Thrilled and shocked at the news, she looks to Sherlock. But with the entire auditorium cheering and clapping, she's immediately bombarded by loads of students cheering and congratulating her.

"Wow! Thank you, guys," she says. "I appreciate it. Thank you." Behind Jane, Sherlock slowly slips away. He sneaks out of the cafeteria and into the Main Hallway. Sherlock closes the cafeteria door behind him and walks down the empty hall. He takes a deep breath.

"I'm impressed," someone speaks. Sherlock spins around to find his older brother, Mycroft. "That was a very selfless thing to do, Sherlock."

"Well. I had help," he responds. "I was told by a very selfless person that I shouldn't only be thinking of myself."

"There is nothing new under the sun, brother. It has all been done before. We're just discovering it at our own pace." Mycroft looks at his watch. "Best get going. See you at home, Sherlock."

And with that, Mycroft walks away, leaving Sherlock alone in the hallway. Sherlock opens the package Jane gave him to see a hat—a deerstalker cap. It has a note that reads: "For you. It matches your style."

Suddenly, Jane's voice comes on the P.A. System. Sherlock opens the door to the Auditorium to peer inside and see her give her acceptance speech.

"Obviously, I hoped I would win this election and thanks to all of you, I did. However, what I couldn't have predicted was that winning class president wouldn't be the best part of my year. Throughout this race, I've made a new friend. He dresses funny and he thinks he's smarter than everyone. And while I think he's got a lot to learn about Brompton Middle School, he showed me that I have a lot to learn about sacrifice."

Sherlock looks at the deerstalker cap in his hands. He walks down the hall, alone, before pausing. "The truth is..." he says to himself as he puts on the hat, "I am smarter than everyone."

I. Ashmawey

39

The White Bull

The White Bull

There once lived three bulls; a white bull, a black bull, and a red bull. The three were friends and very close to each other. Though they were not tied by blood, they didn't feel it lessened their closeness. For they have seen many trials together. When they would find food, they were especially keen on dividing the nourishment equally amongst them.

"Resentment," the White Bull would say, "would be the end of us. Let us never let a foe come between us." A foe, as he would later explain to the Black and Red Bulls, is any evil thought that is carried in the heart. Since what is carried in the heart is not easily altered, such as what enters the mind.

"Why do you refer to it as a foe?" the Black Bull asked.

"Such thoughts wedged between friends almost always come from another entity; a foe," the White Bull responded. "So the idea itself is also a foe."

The three bulls traveled many years together from prairie to prairie. Whenever they would find a good land and settle in it, the Red Bull would frequently become worried. "What if this land dries up?" the Red Bull would ask.

"That would be most unfortunate. What would we do, White Bull?" the Black Bull would add.

"We would then find another land," the White Bull would respond calmly. The Black Bull would nod his head, assured.

"But what if that land becomes dried up as well? What if there are predators? What if..." and the Red Bull would go on.

"We would endure," the White Bull would respond. This was a normal conversation they would visit often. Over the years, their personalities did not change much. For if there is no motivation to change...

Many years passed, and the three bulls grew closer.

One day, after just settling in a new land that was bountiful with plants and herbs, they went down for a long, peaceful sleep. Before falling into their deep slumber, they, of course, had their traditional conversation of optimism versus pessimism. The White Bull gave what energy he had to the Red Bull who took it most willingly, while the Black Bull neither gave nor received.

I. Ashmawey

Deep into the night, searching for food, a wolf watched the three friends breathe deeply as they dreamt. Even though they were sleeping, he knew he could not contend with all three. Even one of them alone would be quite the challenge. Sure, his teeth were strong and sharp. But they were each massive in size with more muscle in one leg than the wolf had in his whole body. Cunning, the wolf thought to himself, "Divide et impera." He would constantly repeat those words in his head, paying more attention to the first. "Divide… divide… divide… divide… and then I shall conquer." He waited till the sun woke up, then he returned to where the bulls grazed. As they enjoyed their breakfast, he crept up and watched them from afar.

He waited.

Waited and waited and waited. He was waiting for something in particular, and then it happened. The White Bull left to relieve himself in the forest. That's when the wolf jumped to his feet and approached the remaining two bulls with his muscles tensed and his back strong. His tail flew up in the air along with his snout. The Red Bull noticed him immediately and quickly called out to the White Bull, but the White Bull was too far. The Black Bull threw his gaze quickly between the Red Bull and the forest, unsure of what to do. The wolf continued his trek to them with his same intimidating posture.

"Stop there," the Red Bull proclaimed with strength. The wolf faltered, slowing down his pace, but still inching forward.

"I'm a friend," the wolf said to them, still moving forward. "If you want me to be."

"We do not want you at all, wolf," the Red Bull spoke with anger. "Leave us!"

"I won't leave you," the wolf responded. He knew he was risking much, but he had studied the bulls' personalities and knew what he was doing; divide and conquer. "Listen to me closely. I have been watching you, my friends. And let me tell you that you cannot continue to travel forever. Eventually, you will tire. And a predator like myself will easily overtake you." The Red Bull thought to himself, it was true! This was his problem with the White Bull's plan of continuous travel all along. "You must find a permanent home and then you will be able to rest comfortably. Nevertheless, there is something else I must say to you two. Just like you must feed, so must I. And my canine teeth are nothing you can match. There are many more of my kind. I would rather not kill you all, I would rather you live happily and peaceful-ly. Nonetheless, today I am here and I must feed. Here is my proposition: let me eat the White Bull, and I will leave you be and move on with my pack. You will not hear from any of us, and you will be safe."

The decision was reached far faster than you may assume. The Red Bull hesitated, but only to make it seem as though he was carefully weighing the options. The Black Bull said nothing, he nodded his head to everything and anything the Red Bull said. Eventually, both bulls agreed, and the White Bull was quickly devoured in the forest.

But as with all wrong decisions, the effects returned to haunt the two bulls soon enough. Time passed, and the wolf became hungry again. For he had never actually left, just waited in the forest long enough to make the bulls believe they were safe. So later when his stomach growled once again, he went to the Red Bull when he was alone and argued that he was ferocious and powerful. If the Red Bull let him eat the Black Bull, he would leave in peace. The Red Bull was furious at first, why was the wolf still there? Did he not promise he would leave? The wolf explained that illness took him for a few weeks and he slept in the forest. Now that he has awakened from his sickness, he needed to feed to strengthen his body. Then he would most assuredly leave. The Red Bull agreed and the wolf murdered and ate the Black Bull.

The Red Bull enjoyed being alone. There was more for him to eat, and no arguing to take place. The Red Bull was at peace.

Though eventually, boredom visited him, then loneliness lifted him, then depression took him away. He was alone in every sense of the word. The Red Bull had much time to contemplate his decisions. Yes he was deceitful, and yes he was selfish, but he was also smart. And so when the wolf came to visit again, the Red Bull was not the least bit surprised.

"You know why I'm here," the wolf said.

The Red Bull said nothing in response. And as the Red Bull saw death in the wolf's eyes, as the teeth dug deep into his neck, the Red Bull moaned with his last breath, "I was eaten the day the White Bull was eaten."

For had they stuck together, the wolf never would have defeated them.

I. Ashmawey

40

The Signing

I. Ashmawey

O ften times when an endeavor is to commence, the process begins with a dream. The dream is most commonly unrealistic. After all, if it was commonplace, why embark on the endeavor to begin with? So it is then this quixotic dream that inspires a plan, and it is the prospects of this dream that supplies drive. Some years ago, fifty-six men did just that.

"We hold these truths to be self-evident…"
"…all men are born equally free and independent."
"…they are endowed by their Creator with certain unalienable Rights,
that among these are Life, Liberty and the pursuit of Happiness."
"…governments derive their just Powers from the consent of the people."

Fifty-six delegates led by five fateful men, Thomas Jefferson, John Adams, Roger Sherman, Robert Livingston, and Benjamin Franklin, did something that few before had the courage to do: they fixed something wrong. You see, when something is wrong, one has two choices: accept it until they die, or fight to the death to change it. Unlike other situations, when something is wrong, there is not a third choice. It would not be an exaggeration to say that the majority of people would choose the first choice, to simply accept things the way they are. But why? Is it because it is easier? That is indubitably what you would hear: it is easier.

But is it? What is more painful: ripping off a Band-Aid, or living with a Band-Aid the rest of your life? A Band-Aid that would get dirty, cause infection, and most assuredly do a lot more harm over the years. By the time the person's life would be ending, they would be so sick and weak, they would actually be looking forward to death. Or, the other option, suffer through a temporary pain and rip off the Band-Aid.

When a civilization of people was being unfairly and unjustly treated by their leader, they decided to take matters into their own hands and emancipate themselves from this tyrant. And thus began the independence of the United States. The date was August 2nd, 1776.

I. Ashmawey

"I never imagined I would take part in penning a letter to the King," Jefferson said.

"Not just any letter, but one of this nature," Sherman added. "My, my, how life takes you along the most unexpected of adventures."

"Only when you seek the adventure, dear friend," Jefferson commented to Sherman before standing up and walking to the front of the room. With every step he took, with every creak in the wood floor beneath his feet, everyone's attention shifted from their neighbors to the front. Thomas Jefferson had a way of making you listen long before he ever spoke. It was not consciously on purpose either, it was simply his natural instinctual demeanor.

He stopped at the front, looking out the window onto the prairie ahead. He looked down to the soil and thought to himself, "In a matter of seconds, this soil will be ours. With some ink on parchment, it will transfer ownership from the tyrants to the believers of independence and freedom." He turned back around to face the fifty-five gentlemen who sat before him.

"My brethren," he began. And immediately, his voice choked. He used all his strength, all his prowess to push back the idea of tears beginning to form. He spent a second contemplating why that word, brethren, affected him so. Perhaps because they initially were anything but brethren. From different sides, from different origins, different philosophies, walks of life, ages, classes, everything. But yet, here they were, coming together and putting aside all differences to fight for one cause in one historical moment. Yes, it made sense that tears would form.

"My brethren," he continued. "I do not have to spend time explaining to you why this moment is substantial in meaning and gravity. I do not care about the past. It is after all, over. We have learned what we have learned from it. Let us instead look to the future.

"This country, my brethren, unlike all other countries to ever exist since the dawn of man, will be a home for any and all who value freedom over anything else. It will be a land for like-minded men, women, and children to live in harmony and peace, progressing mankind, and pursuing happiness and justice for all. But the night is darkest before the dawn, my friends. The night is darkest before the dawn. We will have some hardships ahead. Most of which, the men in this room will not experience in their lifetimes, myself included. Before our descendants can learn to love one another, they will first experience hating one another. They will fight the same fight we fought, it is inevitable. Fighting is imminent... but it mustn't last. Hate will not persevere. Soon after, they will recognize the error of their ways and they will work to cleanse their hearts. And it is then that our country will be the most prosperous... and most loving... nation to exist under God, indivisible, with liberty and justice for all."

Oh, the men cheered. They did not just clap and yell and whistle, they cried and screamed and wept. For the words they heard were everything that they had fought and struggled for. These words were everything to them. As Jefferson walked back to his chair, all those he passed patted him on the back or shook his hand. John Hancock then, as President of the Congress, got up and made his historic move of signing the Declaration of Independence. Jefferson continued sitting on his chair, thinking to himself.

"What troubles you, Thomas?" John Adams asked softly. Jefferson didn't budge, his mind racing and his heart overwhelmed. John waited a bit before speaking again. "Do you... do you doubt the words you spoke?" He had nailed it.

"John," Jefferson began, "your words are true. And it saddens my heart."

"What do you say?!" Adams yelled. To which, Jefferson motioned him to lower his voice. "What words specifically do you feel are not true? Are we not a country that values freedom above all?"

"Assuredly, we are," Jefferson responded.

"Of course! And are we not a country to live in peace, justice, and harmony?"

"I pray we are, of course," Jefferson again responded.

"And are we not to have some trials ahead of us?" Adams asked.

"Yes!" Jefferson responded. "We absolutely will. But... I fear... that these troubles can end in one of two ways. We either come out stronger than before... and if that is the case, we shall prosper. We shall prosper beyond any of our most imaginative, most optimistic dreams."

"And if we don't?"

"If we don't... and if our differences tear us apart... and if we continue to look at some as belonging and some as enemies, then it will be the end of us. We will find ourselves where King George is now, with his people running away from him, starting a new country. We will find the worst of us leading us, and the best of us leaving us. If we do not learn to love one another, John, we will never progress. And we will spend eternity fighting rather than living. Oh, what a waste that would be. What a waste of all the lives paid for our freedom and all the sacrifices. What a sheer and utter waste..."

"Thomas," Adams began, "that will never happen."

The End

I. Ashmawey is a passionate Orange County-based Film and Television Writer widely known for his vivid, emotionally-moving writing style. Throughout his creative career, he has written for a multitude of prominent media outlets like Disney Channel and studios. He has also both written and produced numerous independent films.

Born in the heart of Washington D.C., the creative spark entered Ashmawey's life early on. By the age of 10, he started crafting short stories, resulting in statewide recognition. During middle school, he was the editor of the school newspaper. From a young age, he would see the extraordinary in what the majority deemed as ordinary. Ultimately, this is what drove him to share the unique things he saw through the art of storytelling.

Today, Ashmawey is happy to call his passion a lifelong vocation, and consistently strives to create positive change that will continue to impact people for generations to come.

Ashmawey's personal muses are people of both past and present who yearned to make a difference in the world. He is particularly fond of innovative minds like Walt Disney, Ray Bradbury, and Aristotle.

To receive notice of author events and new books by
I. Ashmawey, sign up at www.ashmawey.com